THE HAUNTING OF EDDIE COMPTON

Martyn Croft

ISBN: 978-0-9559872-1-2

Back cover photo: The author

For the real Jennifer

It's not just what we inherit from our mothers and fathers that haunts us. It's all kinds of old defunct theories, all sorts of old defunct beliefs, and things like that. It's not that they actually live on in us; they are simply lodged there, and we cannot get rid of them. I've only to pick up a newspaper and I seem to see ghosts gliding between the lines. There must be ghosts all the country over, as thick as the sand of the sea .... We are, one and all, so pitifully afraid of the light.

(Ghosts, Henrik Ibsen, 1828-1906)

CONTENTS

1. Back on Track   7

2. A New Job   16

3. First Impressions   30

4. Another Garden   41

5. The Parting of the Ways   51

6. Jenny Gets Some Advice   62

7. Letters   70

8. The Spurs Come to Town   81

9. A Reunion on the Beach   89

10. Tragedy   96

11. The Beginning   107

12. A Ghostly Day Out   118

13. Return to Petersgate   133

14. A Shared Secret   147

15. An Old Friend   154

16. Nightmares   166

17. Déjà Vu   175

18. Invisible and Alone   185

19. I Could Have Been Anything   204

20. A Shady Deal from the Past   214

21. Evil Returns   225

22. Snow   231

23. Wrong Choice   238

24. Another Eden   247

1

Back on Track

Cyril Wilby had been Head of Woodwork and Metalwork at Fenton-on-Sea Secondary Modern School for six years. He had tried hard to ignore the rumours that had been circulating for some time, but it seemed certain that secondary education in the area was soon going to be reorganised, resulting in a huge comprehensive school. Fenton Grammar School was likely to become the upper school and Cyril's school would cater only for pupils aged 11 to 14. He had been reluctant to talk to his wife, Martha, about such a possible merger, as it might also have a bearing on his son's education, let alone the significant change in his own duties and responsibilities that would occur. Cyril's son, Leonard, was halfway through his third year at Fenton Grammar and, though he was far from being an academic star, he had made an enormous number of friends through his sporting ability – he was captain of both the Under 14's football and rugby teams. With all of these considerations beginning to nag him, Cyril eventually decided to broach the subject at teatime one Friday in late February that year, 1965. He was straight to the point.

"We may have to move, Martha."

At first his wife seemed not to have heard Cyril's bold statement and carried on munching on a sandwich.

"I said: we may have to move from Fenton, dear."

The mention of the name of their sleepy seaside town caused Martha Wilby to swallow hard and look directly at her husband.

"Move? Move where?"

"I don't know, but away from Fenton-on-Sea."

"Why? Have we got money problems? Can't we afford the mortgage?

"No, dear. I may have to get a new job."

Silence descended on the Wilby's dining room and Len Wilby was first to break it.

"Why, Dad? Are they giving you the sack?"

"No, son, not exactly, but…."

Martha Wilby went pale.

"So why have we got to move, then, Dad?"

"Have you not heard anything at school, Len?"

"About what?"

"About the two schools merging into one big comprehensive."

"Yeah, a bit. Hempsall said we probably wouldn't be taking any first years next September, but why should that affect you, Dad?"

Len's mum seemed relieved and interjected,

"So will you take them, then, Cyril?"

"Yes, and eventually we'll only have pupils aged eleven to fourteen, while Len's school will teach the older ones."

Len frowned.

"But why do you have to move, Dad?"

"Because I won't be teaching O-levels or CSEs anymore, just the young ones – I would hate it and, besides, I would have to apply for my own job in the reorganisation."

Martha seemed to understand, but Len was not convinced.

"But you'd get it, Dad; you're one of the best teachers they've got. Everyone says so."

"That's not really the issue. I just don't agree with comprehensive education. Bright kids like you, or your friend, Eddie, would initially be in the same classes as the weakest ones. It just won't work. We've always been the best place for the real strugglers."

Len's mum was still deep in thought until her husband smiled and added,

"You know what I mean, don't you, love? You know I would be miserable."

"Yes, I suppose so, but what will you do?"

"Look for another job where they're not likely to go comprehensive until after I retire in just over ten years."

Len didn't seem as worried as much as his dad thought he would be at his suggestion and he asked excitedly,

"Where?"

"I don't know yet, but maybe somewhere near London."

"What, where we used to live?" asked Len.

"No way," said Len's mum. "I'm not going back to the East End."

"No, dear, but I think places like Kent and Sussex have no plans to change for a while yet."

Martha Wilby seemed cheered by that but still had worries.

"What about my job?"

"Shouldn't be a problem – schools are always short of good chief cooks like you and…."

Cyril Wilby paused.

"And what, dear?" asked Martha.

"And you might not have to work at all if I get a better job. I've been thinking of getting into senior management. How does Deputy Head sound to you?"

"Really, Dad?" asked Len.

"Yes, I do most of the discipline now at school. Old Tommy Firth is hopeless at it, and that's another reason why it's not a bad idea to move – Fenton Secondary Modern has been going downhill for a while now."

Martha was smiling genuinely by now and said,

"So I could do more voluntary work?"

"Yes, love," replied her husband and turning to his son, he said,

"And what about you, Len – are you O.K. with the idea?"

"Definitely, Dad. Fenton is such a boring place; being nearer to London would be fantastic, especially if I can get to see Tottenham play at White Hart Lane on a regular basis."

"What about Eddie, son? Would you miss him?"

"I don't think so, Dad. We haven't done much together since last summer and the Devon holiday – he's so much cleverer than me that he seems to have got a lot of new friends in the third year at school."

Len's dad metaphorically breathed a huge sigh of relief as his family became attuned to the idea of the possible move from Fenton-on-Sea and tea concluded calmly with all three of the Wilbys thinking their own thoughts about what the future would hold for them. In his bedroom later, Len would be reminded of his dwindling friendship with his one-time best friend, Edward Compton, with whom he had shared some incredible and fantastic adventures over the previous three years.

'Will I miss him?' he thought. 'Why *had* their friendship diminished? Was it that they didn't want to be reminded of the fantasy world they had both been a part of? Did he himself still believe in phantoms and ghosts? Did his friend, Eddie, still have the same memories? What were those memories?'

All these thoughts aroused themselves in Len's mind that Friday evening – thoughts that had been buried in the deep recesses of his mind ever since his and Eddie's near fatal accident the previous summer. Little had been said between them after they had returned to the reality and normality of Fenton Grammar school in the autumn. He made up his mind that, like times of old, he would pay Eddie a visit the following morning which, being Saturday, would mean that they could spend some time together away from their own separate friends and individual pursuits at school.

Saturday, February the 27th arrived with a hint of an early Spring in the air and Leonard Wilby had a jaunt in his step as he left his house, 7 Lime Tree Avenue, to walk the few hundred yards to 38 Fir Tree Close, the home of his erstwhile friend, Eddie Compton. He hesitated for a moment or two as he stood in front of Eddie's front door. He then gave his familiar rhythmic knock and waited. A few months ago his friend would have opened the door almost instantly, but this time it was Eddie's mum, Ann Compton, who appeared in the threshold.

"Oh hello, Len; haven't seen you for ages. How are you?"

"Fine, Mrs. Compton. Is Eddie around?"

"Yes, come on in."

Eddie had just come downstairs and stood behind his mother in the hall. He looked a little nervous.

"Hello, Len. What's up?"

"Not much, mate. I wondered whether you were doing anything this morning."

"Nothing special. Why?"

"Well, it's such a nice day, I wondered if you'd like to go down town…." Len paused and then continued. "Like we used to."

Eddie didn't look too keen – he and Len hadn't really seen each other outside school since the previous October. What did Len want? He usually spent Saturdays playing football or rugby for the school, so Eddie was curious.

"If you like, Len. I'm not doing anything else."

Ten minutes later and the two boys were heading out of Fir Tree Close. Soon they reached the top of the footbridge over the railway line by Fenton station. By this time normal pleasantries had already been exchanged between the two boys, so when Len stopped walking, Eddie suspected his old friend had something important to discuss.

"I called round today because I wanted to talk to you, Eddie," Len said. "We are still friends, aren't we, mate?"

"Of course we are," replied Eddie. "I suppose it was inevitable we wouldn't see as much of each other after last summer, what with all the different things we do at school."

"I suppose so, but I think it might also be because of what we both went through on those fantastic adventures. I, for one, didn't want to be reminded sometimes of the near misses we had."

"What do you mean?" asked Eddie.

Len smiled and said,

"Well, we've been back in reality for about six months now and I've had no nightmares; nothing strange has happened to me and I like it, so I suppose I've subconsciously tried to avoid you where possible in case it should start again. Deep down, you're still my best friend."

Eddie's eyes looked watery and he said,

"You've always been my best friend too, and you always will be, mate. What happens in school is different."

Len grabbed his friend roughly and gave him a self-conscious hug, before stepping backwards and grinning. The two boys then spent several minutes chatting about the fantastic adventures of the previous two summers. Both were relieved to discover that they each remembered them in exactly the same way, culminating with their narrow escape from being run down by a train while on holiday together with Eddie's mum and dad in Ludmouth in Devon the previous August. Len had one final question before he would give his friend his own news.

"Have you seen any of our friendly ghosts since, or has anything happened to you out of the ordinary?"

"No, mate, to both questions. What about you?"

"Nothing also, apart from the occasional dream of magic carpets and railway tunnels. I still get a bit nervous when I'm at Fenton station and hear the noise from train engines. Thought I glimpsed old Granty wandering the country lanes once when I looked out of the train window on the way back from Hamsden."

Aloyisious St. John Grant had been the elderly owner of Grant's Emporium at the top of Steep Hill. He had tragically died in a train crash the previous year and had made a ghostly reappearance when the boys had been out cycling the country lanes not far from Fenton. His bric-a-brac shop had since been turned into small tearooms with lovely views over the promenade and sea from a small courtyard at the rear. Eddie had only made the twelve mile journey to Hamsden by bus since they had experienced their phantom train journeys the previous summer.

"We seem to have made a good start at trusting reality again, mate," concluded Eddie eventually.

"Yes, but I still wonder if anything like it will ever happen again, you know," said Len. "Do you think it will, Eddie? Do you want it to?"

"That's a 'no' to both, old son. A definite 'NO'."

"I agree. I'll just stick with my dreams like everyone else. Reality is much safer!" said Len finally.

The sun was shining brightly as Len gazed wistfully out to sea from their vantage point on top of the footbridge. He stared into the distance as he thought of his own possible new and bright horizon. Eddie was about to start walking again but Len put his hand on his shoulder and said,

"Eddie, I've got some news."

"What, mate?"

"We're probably going to be leaving Fenton."

"Leaving? Where to?"

"Don't know yet exactly, but my dad wants to leave Fenton Secondary because it will probably go comprehensive. We may go back to somewhere near London, if he can get a job. He wants to be a Deputy Head."

"Oh," said Eddie quietly. "When will you go?"

"Probably July or August if Dad gets a job for September."

"Do *you* want to go, Len?" asked Eddie.

"I think so. I mean, I haven't exactly done very well academically at Fenton Grammar, have I? It would be a fresh start for my O-levels. Dad says it's probably the best time this year."

Eddie was very quiet for the next few minutes as the two boys made their way down the footbridge and into the High Street. They had reached Arleson's the bakers where Eddie's sister, Jenny, worked full-time. Jennifer Compton was nearly nineteen and was going to start a hairdressing and beauty course at Hamsden Civic College the following September. Eddie peered into the baker's window and gave his sister a cheery wave. Suddenly, he turned back to Len and said,

"I shall miss you, mate."

"I shall miss you too, Captain," replied Len with a smile. "It's not the end of the world though, mate. You can come and stay with us after we move. I'll take you to White Hart Lane to watch some real football."

"No thanks, mate!" said Eddie. "That's one thing I shall definitely not miss."

"What's that?" queried Len.

"You going on about Spurs every time football is mentioned. There are other teams, you know."

"Are there? I hadn't noticed," said Len.

By the time the two boys parted company just before lunch that Saturday morning, the old friendship was back on track. What had kept them together as friends from the time when they had been eight-year-olds, seemed stronger than ever: the same humour; the shared experiences of some fantastic adventures and the knowledge that no one else knew what they had been through.

2

A New Job

After only two applications for a Deputy Headship, Cyril Wilby received his first letter requesting him to attend for interview just before Easter on Tuesday, April the 13th. The Banham School was a Secondary Modern School similar in size to Fenton Secondary and was situated in the small seaside town of Petersgate on the north Kent coast about sixty miles from London. The area seemed affluent enough to Cyril when he alighted from the train at Petersgate station that Tuesday morning. It was no more than a five minute walk along a respectable tree-lined avenue leading to the school which was set in a residential area not unlike that surrounding Fenton's two secondary schools. Cyril felt comfortable and relaxed on his walk to the school – he had a good feeling about the job being offered.

He arrived at Banham School's reception at eleven o'clock precisely for his interview scheduled at a quarter past. He quickly discovered that he was the only candidate that day. After a brief tour of the school followed by lunch, the main interviews began at two and ran for exactly two hours. In the final one he faced a panel of five; two female governors, a local authority official, the present Deputy Head and the Headteacher, Mr Peter Boulter. Cyril Wilby emerged from the Head's study at ten past four, exhausted but confident that he had given it his best shot. He was escorted to a waiting room to await the decision. Half and hour later and the Deputy Head came to take him back into the interview room. The panel was still in place. It looked ominous. Mr Boulter motioned to Cyril to sit down and said,

"Mr Wilby, I have one more question for you."

"Yes, Headmaster?" replied Cyril nervously. 'What now?' he thought.

"What would you say if we were to offer you the post of Deputy Head in charge of Pastoral Care, Mr Wilby?"

Cyril Wilby was lost for words.

"Come now, Mr Wilby," interjected the Chair of Governors. "What would you say?"

"What would I say?" stammered Cyril. He hadn't been expecting this. What should he say? He tried to cover himself in case he was still under interview and he was being tested.

"Well, Headmaster. If you were to offer me the post you've just described, then I would say, yes. *Are* you offering me the post?"

Peter Boulter smiled and the rest of the panel seemed to relax at the same time. The Chair of Governors winked at Cyril.

"Of course we're offering you the job, Cyril and I presume by your reply that you accept."

"Yes, Headmaster."

"Peter, please, and congratulations, Deputy Head."

Cyril Wilby retraced his steps along Station Avenue to catch the 5.10 train back to London Victoria. His mind was in a whirl. Had he really said yes? Was he really going to be a Deputy Head from September? How would Martha react? It would be a big change for Len, but he felt that both his wife and son were behind him; this was a family decision. He was in a much more positive mood when he reached the station, so positive that he began planning a mild celebration when he got home. Adjacent to the station was a row of shops and, spotting an off-licence, he hastily purchased a bottle of his wife's favourite wine – a 1963 sparkling Vouvray. It was five past five and he had to run to catch his train, choosing an empty carriage at the front so that he could think undisturbed about his momentous decision.

First stop was the small market town of Faversham where several new travellers joined the train. An elderly man entered Cyril's carriage. He smiled and nodded to the new Deputy Head and sat down directly opposite. Cyril Wilby looked at the old man with some curiosity; he was very smartly dressed, but his clothes were from another era. A deep red cravat, a wide brimmed felt hat, and what looked like riding boots, stood him apart from the usual commuters who frequented the train. Cyril put him down immediately as an actor from a small-town repertory theatre, probably off to an evening performance somewhere. The stranger seemed to be about to start up a conversation but Cyril Wilby closed his eyes as if he needed to snooze after a long day and the flamboyantly dressed old man leant back in his seat and stared out of the window.

The stress and emotion of the day eventually caught up with Cyril and, with the rhythmic vibration from the rails, he soon drifted off to sleep. He was jolted awake when the train pulled into Chatham. The old man had clearly also been asleep as he quickly looked out at the station and said,

"Where are we?"

"Chatham, I think, sir," replied Cyril.

"Oh, that's alright, I thought I'd missed my stop."

"Where do you want?" asked Cyril.

"I change at Bromley for Flixted Town."

The second name meant nothing to Cyril Wilby and he just nodded politely.

"My name's Jacob, by the way," said the stranger. "Jake for short."

Cyril declined the invitation to give his own name; he wanted to keep his own company and carry on with his thoughts of the future. The old man was persistent.

"Where've you come from, sir?"

"Petersgate."

"Ah, I see," said the man knowingly. "And where are you going to?"

"Fenton-on-Sea," replied Cyril Wilby, hoping the old man had never heard of such an out-of-the-way place and that the conversation would dry up. He was soon disappointed.

"Oh really. Now let me see; is the Beach station still open?"

"Beach station?"

"Yes, it was opened in '89 to cater for the new holiday trade."

"What, 1889?"

"Well, obviously. It could hardly have been there in 1789."

The old man smirked. Cyril Wilby said nothing. As far as he knew there hadn't been a second station in Fenton since well before the war.

"So is it still open, sir?"

"No."

The stranger at last sensed that his fellow passenger didn't want to talk and the two men settled back in their seats to concentrate on their own thoughts.

'Bromley, Bromley South'

The old man got up at the announcement from the station platform loudspeaker. He moved towards the door. He suddenly stopped and turned to face his fellow passenger.

"When you move to Petersgate, Cyril, make sure you look after your family carefully."

The old man left the carriage before Cyril had a chance to reply and, though he dashed out of the carriage to call him back, Cyril could not see him on the platform. He had disappeared. Cyril Wilby's heart was thumping. He fell back into his seat and tried to think clearly and logically.

'Even though I mentioned where I'd been, how did he know I was actually going to move to Petersgate? How did he know I had a family? How did he know my name?'

All these questions rushed through Cyril Wilby's brain. He found the last one easy to answer. *Cyril Wilby* was on a label fixed to his brief case. A copy of the day's interview schedule lay face up beside the case, but what about his family? A lucky guess? The bottle of wine? What was wrong with Petersgate to cause the old man to issue his warning?

By the time the train pulled into Victoria, he decided that he had probably been making a meal of an innocent remark. He had overreacted, probably as a consequence of the stress of the day and he might have misheard the old man in any case. Two hours later he arrived at Fenton station and memories of a quaintly dressed old man called Jacob had all but receded into the back of his mind.

Martha Wilby was waiting in the hall when her husband walked in through the front door at a quarter to ten that Tuesday evening. She rushed forward and hugged her husband.

"Well? How did you get on?"

Cyril Wilby put on as disappointed a look as he could and said, "Bad news, I'm afraid."

Martha took a step backwards.

"Oh, I'm so sorry dear. Maybe it just wasn't meant to be."

Her husband smiled. He had his Christmas Day expression on his face – the expression he used every year to convey to his wife that he'd bought her something special. Martha knew at once.

"You got it?"

"Yes."

"Well done, Dad," called Len from behind his mum. "You're the best – I knew you would do it. When will we be moving? What school will I go to? Will…."

"Steady, son, I've only just got the job and it has to be confirmed in writing yet anyway. I'm exhausted and…."

"Give your dad some space, Len," said Martha Wilby. "He's only just got in. And what, dear?"

"And I need a drink – how about a nice bottle of fizzy Vouvray, love?"

"You remembered; it's my favourite. Let's get some glasses and go into the lounge and you can tell us about your day and the new school."

"Can I have some wine, Dad?"

Len's mum frowned.

"Just half a glass with some lemonade; you've got school in the morning."

"Last day before Easter though, so we won't be doing much," said Len with a grin.

Len didn't see his friend, Eddie, until they met up on the way home from school the following day. The last day of term, though hectic, always finished just after lunch and the two boys wandered up South Road in the early afternoon sunshine. As they passed Fenton Secondary Modern, Len stopped and stared for a moment at his Dad's present school. He turned back to his friend and said,

"My dad got a new job yesterday down in Kent, Eddie."

The two boys walked for a few paces while Eddie took in the news.

"So that's it, then; you'll be moving," said Eddie eventually.

"Yep. Dad says it'll probably be early August when we go, if we can get a house by then. We're going down next week after Easter to stay in a guest house while mum and dad look for property. They are going to put Lime Tree Avenue up for sale today or tomorrow."

"Whereabouts in Kent are you going? Is it by the seaside?"

"I think so – it's called Petersgate; nearer to London than Fenton-on-Sea."

"I've heard of that place, you know" said Eddie after a moment. "I'm sure Aunty Carol and Uncle Lionel live near there; I've heard them mention it."

"Where do they live, then?"

"I think it's called Hargate. I'll be able to stay with them if you don't have enough room."

"Excellent, chief."

'Quite like old times', thought Eddie.

"Did you tell your form master, Mr Collins, that you wouldn't be going into the fourth year?" asked Eddie as they reached the corner of Fir Tree Close.

"No, I'll tell him when I go back after Easter. I don't know which school I'll be going to yet. We're going to investigate that as well next week. Dad says that there's an all boys' Grammar School at Faversham and a mixed one in Petersgate itself. I rather like the idea of no girls! Faversham is only one stop on the train from where we're going to live."

The two friends parted company arranging to meet up again in three day's time on Easter Saturday – a trip to Hamsden on the train was the plan, taking in the football game at Freeman Street, the home of Third Division side Hamsden Town, in the afternoon.

Len's dad arrived home soon after his son – his news hadn't been received too well at Fenton Secondary. He would be missed. However,

Martha Wilby had good news for him when he gave her the customary peck on the cheek in their kitchen.

"Mr Donaldson at Walker's says he's already got a buyer for our house, and at the price we want."

"Really," said her husband. "When can they move?"

"Well – and this is the good bit – the husband is a teacher too. He's starting at Fenton Central Junior School in September. They're moving from Cambridge."

Cyril Wilby looked reasonably pleased but had a concern.

"It'll depend on how much property is down in Kent; we may need to extend the mortgage."

"Will that be a problem, then?"

"No, not with my new salary, I suppose. We'll find out next week, hopefully."

"When are we going, Dad? Is it still next Tuesday, like you said?" asked Len as he came in from the lounge.

"Yes, son. We catch the nine-fifteen train."

"You should buy a car, Dad, when we move. We may not be as near to your school as we are here."

"I know, Len. I'd already thought of that and I'm going to see if we can afford to buy one when we get back from Kent."

"Brilliant," said his son.

Len called round for his friend at nine-thirty on Saturday, April the 17th. Eddie was unusually quiet on the way to Fenton station. He and Len often paused at the junction of Fir Tree Close with South Road ever since Eddie's sister, Jenny, had been involved in a car crash there when her boyfriend, Gary Jones, had lost control of his Austin A40 eighteen months ago. Some people believed that Eddie may have saved his sister's life when he pulled her from the wreckage. Eddie had no recollection of the event except the poignant memory of cradling his injured sister on the very pavement where the two friends presently stood.

"Have you forgiven Gary for causing your sister's injuries?" asked Len quietly. He knew Eddie had hated Jenny's boyfriend in the past.

"Yeah, he's O.K. – he's training to be a fireman, you know. The fire brigade was impressed with the way he helped save people in the train crash at Linham Junction last year. Jenny's still besotted with him and he gets on well with my dad now."

Fred Compton had been equally antagonistic to Gary Jones after he had caused his daughter's broken ankle and dislocated shoulder, but following Gary's heroics in the aftermath of the train crash, he had warmed quickly to his daughter's suitor. Eddie's dad was the senior clerk in the booking office at Fenton railway station and had learned of Jenny's boyfriend's deeds first hand. Ann Compton, Eddie's mum, only wanted her daughter to be happy and she'd always known that, despite his faults, Gary Jones gave her daughter confidence and a spring in her step.

The two friends made their way into the High Street and were soon on Platform One and waiting for the ten past ten train to Hamsden. They had ten minutes in hand and Eddie was still quieter than normal. It was also clear to Len that it wasn't just memories of his sister's accident that were the cause.

"What's the matter, mate? You seem preoccupied."

"Oh nothing really. It's just that...."

"Come on, tell comrade Wilby. What's the problem?"

Eddie looked embarrassed, but after a moment he blurted out,

"I haven't been on a train since last year when we both went to London for the day. Since then, when I've been to Hamsden, I've always gone by bus or in my dad's Morris Minor."

"Why?"

Len knew it was a stupid question as soon as he'd asked it. The fantastic adventures they'd experienced when they had been on ghostly trains had clearly put Eddie off rail travel for life, especially after they had narrowly missed being run down by a goods engine when walking on a supposedly disused railway line in Devon the previous summer. He was quick to apologise and put his friend at his ease.

"Sorry. Stupid question, mate."

"That's alright, Len. I've got to put those unreal adventures out of my mind. Sometimes they do seem like a dream to me and that's the way I want to remember them."

"Me too. Just think, Eddie, nothing otherworldly has happened to either of us for at least eight months now, so I think we're back in reality now for good."

"Hope so, chief," said Eddie.

Just then, as if to cement that reality, the train for Hamsden pulled up at the platform and the two boys boarded it for their day out.

Meanwhile that morning, Cyril Wilby had some investigating to do. He hadn't forgotten the strange old man he'd met on the train back from Kent on Tuesday. His parting sentence had kept coming back and it bothered him. *'Look after your family very carefully'*. Had it just been a natural thing to say if the man had guessed Cyril was a family man and about to move to Petersgate? Was he a psychic of some kind, rather than an actor – he had certainly been dressed like one? Cyril had racked his brains all week to try to remember the name of the old man's destination and it had eventually come to him as he lay in bed that Saturday morning.

Shortly after the two boys had boarded the train to Hamsden, Cyril Wilby entered the station forecourt and headed for the booking office. Fred Compton was surprised to see his friend.

"Hello, Cyril. You've just missed Len; he and Eddie have gone to Hamsden."

"Yes, I know, Fred; it's you I want to talk to."

"Oh, where are you off to, then?"

"Nowhere. I just need some information."

Fred Compton was curious – he liked to help people find the best and cheapest ways around England, but Cyril wasn't going anywhere, so what did he want? Cyril Wilby told a little white lie.

"Friend of mine at school is doing some research on railway stations and he needs some information about one down in Kent, Fred."

"Oh yes. Which one?"

"Flixted Town."

Fred Compton looked puzzled.

"Do you know which line it's on?"

"North Kent line; you change at Bromley for it."

"Ah, I think I remember. Just give me a moment."

Fred disappeared into what appeared to be a storeroom at the rear of the office. After a couple of minutes, he reappeared with a broad grin on his face.

"Found it, mate. Flixted Town was a station on the River Medway."

"Was?" queried Cyril.

"Yes, it closed before the war in about 1935 – something to do with a decrease in river trade. You alright, Cyril? You look very pale."

Cyril quickly regained his composure and said,

"One more question, Fred. You know we're moving down to Petersgate in the summer."

"Yes, Eddie told me."

"Well, what do you know about the place?"

Fred looked more curious.

"Nothing really; it's just the next station to Faversham where you can change for Canterbury and Dover, but it's not a significant junction in itself. I don't know anything about the town – why would I?"

"Oh well, my teacher friend will be pleased with the information about Flixted. I better get going."

Cyril Wilby turned to leave, but Fred stopped him.

"Wait a minute, Cyril. I've just remembered something about Petersgate. I'm almost sure I read somewhere in an old railway magazine or something that there used to be a mental asylum there in mid-Victorian times. It was used as an overspill from London. They used special trains to transport them from Victoria – couldn't have other passengers accompanying them, could they? I think it was closed down before the war when ordinary hospitals began to take some of the less serious cases. I did also read that some of them escaped once and that they didn't get all of them back. Apparently nobody knew what happened to them."

Cyril quickly said his goodbyes to Fred and made his way back home to Lime Tree Avenue. He needed to think. As he saw it, there were two possibilities. First, he could have misheard the name of the old man's destination or, second, he had met his first ghost! Being the down-to-earth man that he was, he soon decided that first option was the only possible explanation. He was less worried about the former mental asylum – after all, it had been closed for thirty years. By the time he had reached his front gate his mood had changed for the better. There were no such things as ghosts! As he walked up the path he suddenly remembered that he'd forgotten to ask Fred about the other 'station' – Fenton Beach. It took him a few short seconds to decide he didn't really want to know if and when there had been a station by the beach in Fenton-on-Sea. His family's future was too important and exciting to be worried about ghosts and railway stations from another time. He would make a conscious effort – he told himself – to avoid thinking about his chance meeting with the strange old man; his mind was only playing tricks. He had been very stressed and exhausted that Tuesday evening.

Len and Eddie had a good day together culminating in a 3–0 win for the Town over Seaton United. Both were in good moods on the train journey back to Fenton. The train had just slowed to pass through Linham junction – a speed limit of thirty had been enforced since the tragic crash of the previous year when the Hamsden train had come off the rails, resulting in two fatalities and tens of other casualties. Eddie seemed to be staring at something out of the window.

"Can you see him, mate," asked Len.

"What, Aloyisious, you mean?"

"Of course, who else?"

"Stop it, Len. I thought we'd agreed not to talk about ghosts and phantom trains. Aloyisious St. John Grant died in the train crash and that's that."

"We did see him afterwards, didn't we though?"

"Yes, we did, but it was a one-off – and it was probably all still part of the game we were allowed to play with my train set when we went on all those fantastic journeys. The game ended last summer."

"What about our friend and saviour, Mr Manders, then?" continued Len.

The two boys had narrowly missed being run down by a shunting engine the previous August in Devon. They had both been convinced that a tramp had pushed them out of the train's path at the very last moment, thus saving their lives. The engine driver swore later that there had been no tramp. The ghostly Mr Manders had appeared to them on a previous holiday to the same part of Devon and he seemed to have different guises, from well-dressed to a tramp. Eddie took some time to reply.

"All part of the game, mate. It was to teach us a lesson about believing in reality. We thought the train noise wasn't real because of what we'd been through before."

"But it was," said Len.

"Exactly. We have to live our lives in the real world as we grow up and, just like we eventually gave up believing in Father Christmas, it was a way of ensuring we would be able to. Presenting us with a situation where we faced ultimate danger, I think, was the best way of doing it. Staring death in the face is a great antidote against meddling in the world of ghosts and the paranormal."

Len smiled.

"You've spent a lot of time working that out, haven't you, O wise one!"

"We've had a lot of time since last summer," concluded Eddie finally.

There the matters of ghosts and paranormal experiences would rest until later that summer. In the meantime, it was to be hoped that Len's dad would not share his own experience of ghostly meetings with his son. Leonard Wilby would, perhaps, have been able to offer a solution to the identity of the exuberantly dressed old man from another age, whom his dad had met on the way back from successfully acquiring his new job.

3

First Impressions

The two boys didn't see each other again before the Wilbys were due to go on their exploratory trip to Kent. Both families spent a quiet Easter owing to the atrocious weather that hit the East Anglian coast, although Jenny had her boyfriend Gary's company for Sunday lunch – he was very much part of the family at last. The Wilbys spent some time organising the last minute arrangements for the Tuesday journey by rail. The sun appeared briefly late on Monday after nearly two days of incessant rain and strong winds. By that evening the wind had dropped to a mild breeze and the weather forecast looked good for the following day.

Len and his parents arrived at Petersgate station by mid-afternoon on the Tuesday and after a short taxi ride they checked into their small guest house for their four-night stay. The train journey had been uneventful for Cyril Wilby – no strangers had made themselves known to him. Both Len and his mum were impressed at how clean and well-cared for everywhere seemed to be. After some tea and a change of clothes the Wilbys left *Eastland Court*, their temporary accommodation, and headed for the town centre. Len noticed immediately that Petersgate was larger than Fenton-on-Sea and had a much better array of shops. The residents seemed more affluent as well. To his surprise Petersgate Grammar School was located right in the heart of the town, occupying about a hundred yards of frontage in the main thoroughfare, naively named Front Street. Though he'd previously warmed to the idea of attending the boys' grammar in neighbouring Faversham, he recognised at once the advantages of being at the heart of the town. He wondered if fourth years were allowed out at lunchtime. The school certainly seemed to be soaked in history and tradition as the sign outside main entrance suggested.

Petersgate County Grammar School
Headmaster Mr E.R. Crompton, M.A.(Cantab)
Established 1766
Usque conabor

"Two hundred years old next year," said Len's dad as they walked past the school gates.

"Looks it too," said Len who had spotted the similarity to his best friend's surname. 'This has to be a good sign', he thought. 'I wonder if the Headmaster's first name is Edward'. Len's mum interrupted her son's musings.

"Translate please, Len."

"Sorry, Mum – we haven't come across that."

Even if he had been taught the meaning of the Latin phrase it wouldn't have been much use as the subject was a complete mystery to Wilby Minor – he regularly came bottom in his class in both French and Latin, unlike his friend, Eddie, who always came first or second (a failure). Len's dad couldn't help.

"Didn't do Latin when I was at school."

After leaving the school, Len's mum and dad wanted to spend time visiting the several estate agents and knew that their son would only be a hindrance to their investigations. He was left to wander the town on his own under strict instructions that he rejoined them outside the school gates after exactly one hour. They synchronised watches and Len set off to explore the town.

Apart from buying a couple of postcards – one to be sent later to Eddie – Len didn't find too much else of immediate interest so he decided to make his way back up Front Street to have another look at his potential school. To his surprise one of the main gates was ajar and, plucking up courage, he entered the main grounds. If anyone stopped him he had the perfect excuse – he was hoping to start in September and he was new to the area. The school was much bigger than he imagined with further, and much more modern, buildings on the far side of three parallel rugby pitches. The reason for the gates being open suddenly became clear when a voice called to him from a large hut to his left.

"Hey, you there, what'ya doing?"

A burly, weather-beaten man was approaching. He had all the traditional looks of a school caretaker and a no-nonsense one at that. Len looked apologetic.

"Sorry, sir, the gate was open and…."

"May have been open, lad, but it's not open to you. What year are you in?"

"I don't go to this school yet, sir."

The caretaker seemed to mellow a little.

"You hoping to come here, then?"

"Yes, sir. My dad is going to be the new Deputy Head at Banham Secondary from September."

Bill Weaver was obviously impressed and Len realised for the first time what advantage he might have courtesy of his dad's new job.

"Have you seen Mr Crompton yet and it's Bill by the way?"

"Not yet. Dad only got the job a week ago and we're on holiday until May the 4th."

"We go back on the 3rd. You can tell your parents that. Just get them to ring Mrs Wilkinson in the office – she deals with all new applications. Where are you coming from?"

"Fenton-on-Sea."

"Never heard of it. Are you at a grammar school there, then?"

"Yes, a mixed one in Fenton."

"Shouldn't be a problem, then – I think there are plenty of places available in the fifth year. Had to get rid of a few, you know."

"I'm only fourteen, Bill, so I'll be starting in the fourth year."

"Hm, you look older, lad. What's your name?"

"Leonard Wilby, Len for short."

"Well, Len, I'll look forward to seeing you in September. Anything else you want to know now?"

"Do you play football?"

"Football, rugby and cricket; one term of each."

Len smiled; he felt at home. Bill Weaver began to show him the way out but Len had one more question which he wasn't sure he dared ask. However, he just came straight out with it. The caretaker had seemed friendly enough.

"What does the 'E' in Mr Crompton's name stand for?"

Len felt immediate relief when his question was clearly not perceived to be impertinent. Bill Weaver smiled.

"Never really been sure, but just between you and me, Len, we call him Teddy, but I don't know if it stands for Edward as usual or not. You'll see why it might just be a nickname when you meet him. It'll have to be our secret; I'm only allowed to address him as Mr Crompton."

That sealed it for Len; it was a good omen. He would constantly be reminded of his best friend. He had to go to this school.

Len emerged from the school grounds and found his parents waiting for him on the pavement outside. He was ten minutes late and they looked anxious.

"Where have you been?" asked his mother with some surprise.

"Oh, just talking to the caretaker, Mr Weaver."

"And is this the school you think you'll be going to, then?" said Cyril Wilby. "Have *you* made the decision?"

Len couldn't tell from his dad's tone whether he was genuinely cross or just being his sarcastic self.

"Looks a good school, Dad, and they've got places in the fourth year. Bill says so."

"Bill?"

"Sorry, Dad – Mr Weaver, the caretaker."

Len's dad's apparently stern face seemed to break into a pleasant enough smile.

"So you think you've made a good choice, do you, son? Did you go right to the other side of the school?"

"No, I just stayed by the main building while I talked to the caretaker."

"What did you see the other side of the playing fields?"

"How do you know there are playing fields, Dad?"

"Because, my son, the Banham School backs on to Petersgate Grammar; the sports pitches are often shared by the two schools."

Cyril Wilby put on his serious face again.

"Therefore, young man, I do not think it's a good idea for you to be so close to me; I have a reputation to create. Faversham Boys' Grammar would be a much better choice."

"But, Dad…."

"No buts, son."

This time Len was convinced that his dad was deadly serious and, trying not to show his disappointment, he walked behind his parents in silence down Front Street and into the town. He fought back the tears that demanded release. Martha Wilby could sense that her only son was upset and just beyond the end of the main school buildings she turned round – she couldn't keep up the pretence any longer.

"Your dad's only joking, Len. He wanted to be sure that you really do want to go to Petersgate Grammar. Mr Dalby at the estate agents told us that the school is respected by everyone in the town."

Meanwhile, Cyril Wilby had walked a few yards on in front and now stood with a cheeky grin on his face staring at his son. He waited while Len and his mother rejoined him and said,

"Almost an April Fool's joke, eh, son?"

Len was beaming. He punched his dad playfully in the ribs.

"Of course," his dad continued, "you'll have to come down again for interview and trust that they accept your less-than-illustrious academic record to date. You will have to hope that they will be impressed by your captaincy of both the football and rugby teams."

Len's smile contracted a little. His mother had other news.

"We'll have no problem finding a house. There are plenty on the market and at more or less the same price as back home. Your dad has details of five we can see over the next two days. You will have an equal say in what we choose."

'A bigger bedroom', thought Len. Everything seemed to be falling into place and, when his parents announced that fish and chips were on the agenda for later on, he was in seventh heaven.

The next two days were spent mostly visiting properties in and around Petersgate, which Len found slightly boring despite his mum's assurance that he would be able to give his opinion. By Friday morning it was apparent that his parents had agreed between themselves that they would make an offer on 23 The Park, a modest semi-detached situated less than half a mile from the two secondary schools. It hadn't been Len's first choice – his prospective bedroom was only marginally larger than his present one. It did, however, have an enormous garden, mostly laid to lawn – perfect for a small football pitch. His favourite had been on the outskirts of town and was detached. His dad said it was just too expensive and was on a busy main road. The Park was an area of town not unlike the avenues surrounding Fenton station where the Wilbys currently lived. It would be perfect for Martha Wilby as St Michael's Church was located halfway between The Park and the town. Two votes to one swayed it and, after a little negotiation, the Wilby's offer was accepted late that Friday afternoon. The elderly vendors would wait until August for completion – they were moving in with their son and daughter-in-law in Faversham. Cyril Wilby was relieved to discover that the increase needed in the mortgage would be much less than half that which he had been expecting. Solicitors, Edwards and Gilham in Fenton, would be informed the following Monday after the Wilby's return from Kent at the weekend. Contracts for sale and purchase would then be drawn up. The family would return to Kent at a later date to secure Len's place at Petersgate Grammar; the end of May being the most likely time.

Monday the 24th of May came round very quickly for Len. It was the day he and his mum would visit his prospective new school for interview while his dad spent some time at Banham Secondary. Len and Eddie had continued to associate with each other out of school, even though both of them continued to have their separate circle of school friends. Eddie's mathematical ability was again put to good use as scorer for the Under 14's cricket eleven where Len was one of the main batsmen. After the school game on the Saturday before the Wilby's trip to Kent, Eddie wished his best friend good luck.

"You'll get in, just concentrate on the sport, mate and anyway I've got some information for you."

"What?"

"I've translated the school motto for you."

"Where did you get that?"

"I had a peek at their magazine they sent you when I came round to your house last Saturday. I thought at least you ought to know what the motto means."

"And?"

"Well it's what you've got to do on Monday. It means '*I will do my best*'. Just get it into the interview with the Head somehow."

"Thanks, Edward, you're a real friend."

This false formality sparked a memory for Len of his last visit to Petersgate Grammar School and he continued,

"Do you know what the Headmaster's name is, Eddie?"

"Mr Wilby?"

"Close, mate. It's Mr Crompton and his first name might be Edward. Apparently those in the know call him Teddy."

"Dad calls me Ted sometimes, Len," said Eddie finally.

After the two boys parted that Saturday afternoon, Eddie became a little troubled by the strange similarity between his own name and that of his friend's prospective Headmaster. He quickly decided, however, that coincidences like that happened all the time. He was back in the real world now and for good.

'Teddy' Crompton welcomed Len and his mother into his study and Len could immediately see the reason for the moniker. Mr Edward Crompton was rotund and had a full head of curly brown hair; he was about fifty and he had a smile that made you want to cuddle him. Boys at Petersgate

Grammar School soon found that the aura was a perfect disguise for the strict disciplinarian that he actually was.

"So this is Leonard Wilby," he said to Martha Wilby.

"Yes, Mr Crompton," replied Len's mum nervously. She felt as apprehensive as her son. There was something about this Headmaster's eyes that seemed to look right inside you, she thought.

"And is your husband not with you, Mrs Wilby?"

"No, he's taken the opportunity to visit his new school – he's going to be Deputy Head there from September," she said proudly.

"Yes, I know – word soon gets round, you know, but it's a pity he's not here."

"He hopes to join us later," said Martha quickly.

Mr Crompton nodded and he turned his attention to her son.

"So young man, what talents can you bring to this school?"

Len stammered,

"I don't know, sir," and then after a moment's pause he said, "I'm captain of our Under 14's football and rugby teams."

"Really, and do you think that will help you pass your examinations and get you a good career?"

Len looked blank, but then remembered what Eddie had said to him two days earlier.

"The discipline and structure of sport helps me try to do my best at everything else including my studies, sir," and again he hesitated. "Like your school motto says: '*I will do my best*', and as captain I have to lead by example as well."

Martha Wilby's face widened in surprise. Was this her son talking? Her moment of maternal pride was soon curtailed when Mr Crompton said,

"Your academic record, however, doesn't suggest that you've been very successful at converting your prowess on the games field to your academic studies, does it, young man?"

Len was ready with his answer – he'd had plenty of time to think of it on the way down in the train that morning. Cyril Wilby was not due to pick up his new car until they got back to Fenton.

"No it doesn't, sir, but I always try my best; I can't do more."

"Ah, but that's the question isn't it? Is your best good enough for you to come here?"

Len's mum was visibly nervous but her son proved his worth again.

"I think so, sir – after all, I did pass the eleven-plus and I have made some improvements this year. There are at least half a dozen weaker than me at Fenton Grammar."

Although the Head's facial expression didn't change, inside he was impressed with Len's boldness and perception. There was something about this young man that said, Head Boy in three years time. He sat back in his swivel armchair and at last he smiled.

"Well, young man, we'll have to see, won't we? For the time being I think you should take a good look at us to see if Petersgate Grammar will suit you. I'll get Mr Simpson to take you both on a tour of the school. Mr Simpson is Head of P.E. and also the First Year – he'll be able to answer any of your questions."

Two hours later and with both his mum and dad in attendance, Len was back in the Head's study for the decision on his future school. 'Teddy' Crompton wasted no time in conveying it to the Wilbys.

"You'll be pleased to know that I can offer your son a place in our Fourth Year from September."

Len's mum and dad smiled and could hardly raise a 'thank you'. Len was straight to the point.

"Thank you, sir. I won't let you down."

"I hope not, Leonard," said Mr Crompton, sternly. "I hope not."

4

Another Garden

It was late June before Cyril Wilby finally decided on what car to buy. He
had tried several garages in the area including Steve Paton's Autos on
South Road, the closest to his home in Lime Tree Avenue. He hadn't
been behind the wheel of a vehicle since his National Service days and
he'd only driven army jeeps and trucks then anyway. If he was honest he
didn't want to have a car – he'd always walked or cycled to his job at
Fenton Secondary Modern and he'd never seen the need for one.
However, he knew that with the move to Kent and his son growing up
quickly, the family needed independent transport – a Deputy Head had to
have a car, his wife insisted.

Jennifer Compton's boyfriend, Gary Jones, no longer worked for
his dad, Richard, at the second-hand car showroom in Hamsden. Thus it
was with some surprise that Cyril and Martha Wilby were greeted by the
young trainee fireman at about ten-thirty on Saturday, June the 26th.

"Hello, Mr and Mrs Wilby – looking for a car?"

"Yes, Gary. What are you doing here?"

"Just helping my dad out. He's quite busy at this time of the year.
I'm not on call this weekend."

The Wilbys walked further into the showroom and Gary followed
attentively.

"What kind of car were you looking for, Mr Wilby?"

"Not really sure, Gary; something for a family with reasonable
luggage space. Martha here says it has to be red. I'm not bothered about
speed; I just want it to be economical and easy to drive. Though I passed
my test when I was with the army doing my National Service, I haven't
driven for some years."

"I see," said Gary. "We have a nice red two-year-old Vauxhall Victor. It has only done 17,000 miles."

Gary led them to a corner of the showroom where they found the nominated car. Martha's eyes lit up when she saw the gleaming and highly polished paintwork; the chrome wheel hubs shone brightly in the summer sunshine that cleverly illuminated Richard Jones' showroom. Cyril was not too sure.

"It's bigger than I wanted, Gary. How fast is it?"

"Oh it'll cruise comfortably at seventy – it's got a 1500 engine. She's beautiful, isn't she?"

"How much is it?" asked Cyril hoping it would be out of his price range. His wife seemed to be in a trance as she clung to his arm. He could feel her egging him on.

"Well, new, they're over eight hundred. It's the Victor Deluxe."

Cyril breathed a sigh of relief; he only had five hundred to spend. Martha relaxed her grip.

"But…."

Gary paused and pretended to do some mental calculations. He knew he would have to ask his dad for a price, but he wanted his potential customers to think that he knew exactly what he was doing.

"But?" queried Martha Wilby.

"But I'll just have to check one or two things with my father. I haven't got the latest second-hand guide out here in the showroom. Can you just wait a moment please?"

Gary's dad appeared from the office and took over the potential sale.

"Mr and Mrs Wilby? I don't think we've met; I'm Richard Jones. Gary, a coffee for our customers please."

Gary looked cross. They were *his* customers, but, as usual, his dad had taken over. He knew why he had joined the fire service and not followed his dad into the family business! He went to make the coffees.

The experienced salesman's technique was quickly put into practice. No mention of price. Richard Jones opened the passenger door for Martha.

"Take a seat, Mrs Wilby. Try her out for size and comfort."

Cyril Wilby climbed in beside his wife and sat in the supple leather seats. Martha looked like a little girl with her best ever birthday present. She gave her husband a kiss on the cheek. Cyril would have no choice.

"Start her up, sir," said Richard Jones.

Cyril turned the key and depressed the accelerator slightly. The engine purred into life. His last remaining hope was that it would still be out of his price range. He and Martha climbed out of the car and Cyril made a great pretence of inspecting the pristine bodywork for scratches and marks. He would find some fault with it, he hoped, but there was none. The tyres seemed to have little wear on them too. Cyril was all but defeated.

"How much is it, Mr Jones?"

Richard Jones grinned broadly. Another customer in the palm of his hand, he thought. He rarely displayed prices on his cars; it was essential that the customer fell in love with the car first. Then the price didn't matter. It worked every time.

"List price new is eight-two-five, Mr Wilby, but since it's the end of the month I can let you have it for, shall we say, six hundred."

Cyril Wilby shook his head and started to walk away. Martha didn't move and, instead, she took over the negotiations.

"Too much, Mr Jones – this car's two years old."

"Twenty-one months actually – it was first registered in September '63."

"We've only got five hundred, I'm afraid; such a shame."

To both men's surprise Martha Wilby rejoined her husband who had already moved towards the door. Just as she did so Gary called out,

"Coffee's ready."

Gary's dad strode after his lost customers and said,

"Please have some coffee before you go. Perhaps I can offer you a better deal too."

Martha Wilby released her grip on the door handle and turned back to face Mr Jones. She smiled knowingly. It had worked.

Once the Wilbys were seated in the back office, Richard Jones made great fuss of sifting through some papers, most of which were irrelevant to the matter in hand.

"The best I can do for you is five-sixty and that's my very best offer."

Cyril shook his head, but in his mind he had already admitted defeat. That had happened when Martha had planted a kiss on his cheek. She spoke for them both.

"We could go to five-twenty, couldn't we Cyril?"

"Yes, I suppose so," replied her husband with resignation.

Richard Jones sifted through a few more papers and said,

"I'll meet you halfway – five-forty and that's my final offer. Take it or leave it. You're robbing me at that too."

"We'll take it, won't we love?" said Martha.

"Yes, dear – provided you tax it for a year, Mr Jones," responded Cyril; his manhood eventually preventing him from allowing his wife to be able to boast afterwards that she had done all the negotiations.

"It's a deal. You have just bought a car, Mr Wilby. Well done!" said Mr Jones with some relief.

A week later, and with all the paperwork complete, Cyril and Martha Wilby drove off Richard Jones' forecourt in their shiny red car. Despite his lack of recent driving experience Cyril seemed to cope well with both the car's idiosyncrasies and Hamsden's Saturday morning traffic. They were soon on the A132 dual carriageway and heading back to Fenton-on-Sea. Reaching the straight stretch near Linham, Cyril applied more pressure to the accelerator and the Vauxhall cruised smoothly to seventy.

"Don't go so fast, dear. I thought you didn't like speed," said Martha.

"Sorry, love – didn't realise how fast I was going; it's so smooth."

Cyril Wilby eased his foot and the big car slowed to fifty-five and within ten minutes they had pulled onto the drive of number 7 Lime Tree Avenue to be greeted by their excited son.

"Wow, Dad!" exclaimed Len as the Wilbys got out of their new possession. "You'll have to clear the garage out more than you have done; it's bigger than I imagined."

Len was clearly dressed to go out somewhere and his mother said,

"You off to Eddie's, then?"

"Yes, Mum – I'll be out for most of the day. Eddie says he wants to do some things for old times' sake since we're moving in just over three weeks."

The Wilby's move was scheduled for the week after term was due to finish on July the 23rd. The removal firm had pencilled in the 29th and 30th for the two-day move. Len's dad didn't seem too pleased.

"We really need you to help with packing this weekend, you know. What does Eddie want to do that's going to take all day?"

"Don't know, Dad. He just said that there wouldn't be many more times to do all the old things we used to do on a Saturday – there's only three after today and I'm playing cricket on one of them."

"Well, you make sure you're back by five and then you can start sorting your wardrobe and bedroom out."

"Yes, Dad. See you later," and Len was already on his way out of the front gate.

On the way over to his friend's house he pondered the possibilities for the day. He didn't really know what Eddie wanted to do. It wasn't often that they had *all* of a Saturday together owing to his sporting commitments, but Eddie had insisted that they might need several hours. With his dad's curfew in place Len reckoned they had six or so. As he approached number 38 Fir Tree Close a distant memory came to the forefront of his mind. He suddenly had an idea what Eddie wanted to do and it made him very, very nervous. His worst fears were confirmed when Eddie's mum showed him through into the Compton's back garden where Eddie already had part of his plan in place.

"What'cha, comrade Len," said Eddie jumping to his feet. Ann Compton had already disappeared back through the French doors into the house. Len just stared at what was laid out on Fred Compton's neatly manicured lawn.

"Oh no, Eddie. We're not playing with your train set. No way!"

"Oh come on, Len – just one more time for old times' sake."

The two boys hadn't played with Eddie's *Flying Scotsman* train set for well over a year, not since the last fantastic train journey they'd been on just before Easter 1964. The magical train set, as Eddie called it, had been a present from the mysterious Mr George Canter who had owned the junk shop in Mill Road and had been the instigator of the boys' first fantastic journey two years previously.

"No, Eddie. We might end up anywhere and not get back this time. I have to be home by five."

"Len, it's only five past eleven now. We've loads of time and anyway, we're not in my dining room now; it's bright sunshine out here."

"But you know what might happen – we could be transported anywhere and to another time and be left to find our way back like last time," said an exasperated Len.

"Please, Len. Just for old times' sake."

Something in Eddie's tone made Len eventually relent. Was a greater power at work again?

"Oh alright, mate, but just once. It's too nice a day to be messing about with electric train sets."

Eddie grinned playfully. He picked up the controller which was plugged into his dad's extension lead powered by a socket just inside the French doors to the lounge. The wooden tunnel made by Len's dad was in place over one of the two straight sections of track that formed the sides of the large oval layout. Eddie pushed the switch and the engine and its four carriages moved smoothly away. A second or two later and it entered the tunnel for the first time in fifteen months. Both boys watched nervously. It emerged intact and without any apparent loss of time. Len seemed relieved; Eddie looked disappointed. Eddie kept the power on for three or four more circuits but nothing unusual happened causing Len to remark,

"The magic's gone, thank God."

"You try it, then," said Eddie.

Len shook his head, but his friend was insistent and he passed Len the controller. This time the train entered the tunnel and disappeared. Len dropped the small black box. Eddie gasped.

"It's gone! The magic still works!"

Suddenly, as if a total eclipse of the sun had taken place, the Compton's garden was pitched into utter blackness. Eddie screamed.

"Where are you, Len?"

There was no reply. Suddenly, as quickly as the pitch darkness had descended on the garden so it lifted in an instant to bright watery sunshine. Eddie was still kneeling on the grass but it wasn't his garden and Len was nowhere to be seen. He looked round nervously. He was in a very large garden, maybe three times the length of that at 38 Fir Tree Close, Fenton-on-Sea. It was lined on one side by a row of tall conifers with shrubs and flower beds dotted randomly on the other. He could hear voices from a small patio area at the far end of the lawned area. He approached tentatively. Where was Len? An elderly couple was drinking tea. It was late afternoon and summer seemed to be over.

"Excuse me," said Eddie. "Have you seen my friend?"

The two pensioners ignored Eddie's question. He thought the woman seemed familiar; the man did not. He repeated his question. They looked right through him. They were both blind. Suddenly the lady got up from her seat and turned to her husband.

"Finished with your cup, dear?" she said.

"Yes, my love."

The elderly man handed his wife his china cup and she turned back to face Eddie. He thought she was going to hug him but instead she seemed to pass right through him. She then walked back up the lawn to the large semi-detached house, defying Eddie's assumption of her disability. Her elderly husband sat back in his chair and closed his eyes. Despite his age, his clothes seemed fairly modern; it was at least 1965, thought Eddie as he sat down beside him. He stretched out his arm and carefully put his hand right through the old man's head. It confirmed what Eddie had been thinking. The elderly couple were ghosts from sometime in the future.

Eddie sat and waited for the lady of the house to reappear. After five minutes or so and with her husband snoring loudly, Eddie stood up. He would go and investigate where she was and, indeed, where he was. Instantly the blackness returned and he fell to his knees. A few seconds later and the summer sunshine returned. His friend was kneeling beside him with a comforting arm round his shoulder.

"What happened, Len? Where have I been?" cried Eddie.

"Nowhere, mate. You didn't move."

"But it went pitch black, Len."

Len gave his friend an odd look.

"No it didn't. It's been sunny all the time. You just seemed to go into a trance, but your eyes were open. When the train disappeared I dropped the controller and you screamed. A few seconds later and the train reappeared. You've been in suspended animation for about a minute in all I should say."

Eddie glanced down. The engine and four carriages were stationary on the track.

"But, Len...."

But Eddie didn't finish what he was going to say. He knew his down-to-earth friend wouldn't believe him. What could he say anyway? '*Oh I've just been to another garden sometime in the future and in a different place where I met two elderly ghosts*'. He thought not.

The two boys packed Eddie's train set away quickly and in silence. They both realised that their fantastic adventures might not be over despite the gap of almost a year. Len told his friend later that it had been a mild event at best (or worst) and could be explained by a trick of the light. Eddie, of course, thought otherwise but, as before on occasions, he kept his otherworldly experience to himself. Was he going mad? Was there something wrong with him that caused him to see things that weren't there? He would find out later the reason for the visit to the strange garden when he would see it again in tragic but all too real circumstances.

Len was home much earlier that day than expected – he and Eddie had spent a couple of hours in town and on the beach, but both found that they could not easily relax and do all those things that Eddie had planned. It was to be the last time that they would have a chance to skim pebbles on the sea, play the one-armed bandits on the pier or look for amber on the beach.

Eddie tried to put the ghostly time travel out of his mind that Saturday, but something kept nagging him about the identity of the elderly phantoms. He was sure he had recognised one of them – the woman's voice had been familiar, though she had been much older than when he'd last heard it. Len was fortunate that he was able to concentrate on the reality of his family's move to Kent by sifting through and filtering his possessions in his bedroom.

5

The Parting of the Ways

The following three weeks were very hectic for the Wilby family. What with farewell parties for both Cyril and Martha from their colleagues at Fenton Secondary Modern School and the inevitable packing and repacking at home, they hardly had a moment to consider or dwell on their move. Brown's Removals had finally decided that they could accomplish the 150 mile assignment in one day on Friday the 30th of July. The Comptons had arranged a small leaving party for Cyril, Martha and Len on the previous Saturday at Fir Tree Close, three days after the last day of the school term on the Wednesday. The two boys met as usual on the morning of the party – Len called on his friend at Fir Tree Close at nine-thirty. It would be the last Saturday that they would meet together. The Saturday routine had been in place for over six years from the time that Len had first moved to Fenton-on-Sea when the boys had both been eight. Eddie was waiting by his front gate. Len was riding his bike.

"Good morning, Comrade Len."

"Good morning to you, Captain Eddie," replied his friend as he dismounted from his new racing bicycle – a present from his parents for getting a place at Petersgate Grammar School.

The two friends hugged each other almost involuntarily. It was beginning to dawn on both of them how much they would both miss each other. Len clearly had a plan for the morning. The Wilbys were invited at three and Eddie had to be back by one at the latest.

"I thought we might cycle out to Linham Junction, mate," said Len when the embarrassment of the slightly unnatural clinch had worn off.

"Linham? Why?"

"I need to lay a few ghosts; one in particular."

"You mean old Granty."

"Yes, Aloyisious St John Grant, late of this parish."

"Why?" asked Eddie nervously.

"Because, like you when you had to play with your train set one last time, I want to see if his ghost is still walking the lanes near Linham."

Eddie knew that they could be playing with fire if Len's plan resulted in something similar to what he'd experienced when he had been transported to the other garden.

"I don't think that's a good idea, Len," he said.

"Why?"

"Because, I haven't forgotten the episode with my train set only three weeks ago. That's why."

"But nothing happened, mate. I'm not even sure that the train disappeared – you just panicked and hallucinated."

Eddie debated whether to tell his friend about his visit to the strange garden and the two elderly ghosts, but he knew Len wouldn't believe him. A cycle ride was only a cycle ride as well. Why shouldn't they do it? He had to trust reality otherwise he would go mad. He gave in.

"You're right, Len. What could possibly happen on a simple cycle ride?"

"Good man; get your bike and let's saddle up, Mr Merckx!"

The weather began to deteriorate slightly as the two boys cycled into South Road and headed for the roundabout leading to the A132. Linham Junction, the scene of the train crash in which Aloyisious St John Grant had died the previous April, was located between five and six miles from Fenton-on-Sea depending on which route was taken. Len and Eddie would take the back roads avoiding the main road to Hamsden. By the time they had turned left at the roundabout and were a mile or so into the maze of lanes that twisted and turned to their destination, it had become unseasonably chilly and quite dark for the time of year. They stopped briefly at a four-way crossroads and debated whether they should carry on. They were halfway there. Eddie was still not keen and he thought he had the perfect excuse to turn back.

"Come on, Len, it's going to tip it down in a minute. It looks like thunder too."

"Weather forecast was for warm sunshine all day – I checked before I set off this morning."

Eddie glanced in the direction of Linham and it appeared that his friend was accurate in his report. The black clouds directly above them seemed to be encircled by clear blue sky and their destination was in bright sunlight. It wasn't raining.

"O.K., mate. It'll probably be only a shower," concluded Eddie with some reluctance. They took the right-hand road and pedalled furiously towards Linham reaching the level crossing – near where the tragic accident had taken place – in just over ten minutes. As on the previous occasion, Len boldly wasted no time in negotiating the two pedestrian gates and crossed over the line. Eddie hesitated fully expecting his friend to disappear into thin air.

"Wait, Len!" he shouted. Immediately, Eddie was pitched into complete darkness. He couldn't see a hand in front of his face.

"Oh God, it's starting again," he murmured to himself. "Like before in the garden."

He knew he had no choice and he fumbled and stumbled his way across the line, listening intently for the sound of any approaching train. He reached the other side and stood with his bike on the continuing road. The blackness lifted. The dark clouds above him were nowhere to be seen. It was bright sunshine again. Len stood grinning a few yards in front of him. Eddie breathed a sigh of relief as his eyes became accustomed to the bright light. He knew he had to ask his friend what he'd seen, but he sensed it had not been the same as his experience.

"Did it go pitch dark for you, Len?"

"No, mate. As soon as I crossed over the clouds just disappeared. You seemed to have great difficulty following me, like you were blinded by something; sun must have been in your eyes. It was pretty bright after the dark clouds."

Eddie smiled. He would not tell his friend what he'd experienced. There was no point in upsetting him before his imminent move to Kent. Keeping back such information, however, soon became pointless as Len said,

"Look over there. It's different from last time."

Further down the road behind Len, a huge complex of modern concrete and glass buildings glinted in the bright sunshine. They seemed to extend for several hundred yards in all directions. Eddie's jaw dropped. They were not in 1965. The road was much wider than when they'd arrived a few minutes earlier. The sun had clearly just risen above the horizon; it was early morning and no one else seemed to be about.

"Oh God!" he exclaimed. "We've gone into the future."

Len had already read the large signs posted on either side of the road about fifty yards further on.

Bexham Nuclear Power Station
Serving the community since 2010

Neither boy said a word. They were torn uncomfortably between exploring further and turning back to recross the railway line. Suddenly they spotted a tall man approaching from the direction of the power station. He looked to be about sixty and walked athletically. He shouted to them,

"Wait a minute, boys."

Eddie had a déjà vu moment when he thought he recognised the stranger's voice. Len seemed excited.

"What's up?" he asked.

"You can't come any further; you should not have crossed the railway line. There are signs. You cannot miss them. Now go back."

The voice echoed inside Eddie's head. He thought he'd guessed who the stranger was. Len was undisturbed but such thoughts and said simply,

"Sorry, sir. Come on Eddie let's go."

Len turned his back on the strange man and began wheeling his bicycle across the line. Eddie was still rooted to the spot as the man came to within a couple of feet. He had a white coat on with a lapel badge. Eddie read it. It immediately provided the catalyst that spurred him into action. He turned and fled, pushing his friend out of the way in order to escape the terror that was forming in his mind. He and his bike fell onto the road the other side of the line. He was joined quickly by a bemused Len, who shouted,

"Here, watch it, mate. What on earth's wrong?"

Eddie sat up and lied,

"I thought he was going to grab me or worse."

"He looked friendly enough to me, Eddie – a nice old boy."

The two friends stood up and, after dusting themselves down, Len said,

"The magic still works; another ghost, eh?"

Eddie's mind was in a whirl. What could he say?

"Not old Granty, though," he managed. "We must have moved fifty years into the future."

"Shall we go back?" asked Len.

"No way, mate. Not in a million years! We're tampering with the unknown. It's not right."

"I was only joking, Eddie."

The two boys wheeled their bikes away from the phantom scene. They were back in the mid-morning summer sunshine. There was not a cloud in the sky. Len was brave enough to turn round and stare across the railway line. It looked exactly like it had been when they had arrived about ten minutes previously. No nuclear power plant and no strange man. They had glimpsed into the future. Len shrugged his shoulders and mounted his bike. Eddie followed. The lapel badge flashed into his mind. It had read: '*Dr Leonard Wilby*'.

The two boys rode home in almost complete silence. Eddie tried to make sense of what he'd seen. What did it mean? Would his friend end up working at a nuclear power station? Where was Bexham? His brief glimpse at the countryside surrounding the phantom power station had suggested it wasn't in East Anglia. Final questions entered his head: Why had his friend appeared to him as a ghost? Did it mean that he was…?

Both boys continued to be rather subdued at the Compton's garden party later that afternoon prompting Eddie's mum to ask,

"Are you alright, Eddie? You seem rather quiet."

"I'm going to miss Len, Mum. That's all."

"Of course you are, but you'll see each other again. You both seem to think that this afternoon is a bit of a wake. Now come on, for goodness sake, cheer up."

Eddie forced a smile.

"Yes, Mum."

Eddie wandered to the bottom of the garden where his friend also seemed to be preoccupied. The ladies had repaired to the kitchen to prepare the party food. Fred and Cyril were talking cars on a bench near the house. The boys were reasonably out of earshot. Len gave his verdict on the morning's strange experience.

"We weren't near here, you know, after we crossed the railway line, Eddie."

"I know. The scenery was too hilly and it didn't feel as though it was close to the sea."

Len then asked the question that Eddie was dreading.

"Who was the old bloke – the one that stopped us going into the power station? I'm sure I've never seen him before. It wasn't Ally Grant, I'm certain."

"No," said Eddie quietly.

"What did it all mean, mate?" asked Len.

Again Eddie was short with his reply.

"Don't know."

Len continued.

"I reckon it's an omen or something – a pointer to something that's going to happen in the future. It was at least 2010, so I expect we'll have to wait a long time to find out, eh? It's another forty-five years, at least. We'll both be getting old, mate."

Eddie's heart was racing. He didn't reply and he turned away from his friend. Len wondered what was wrong.

"Did it upset you, Eddie?"

Eddie knew he had to change the subject. He couldn't share his secret with his friend. He thought about Len's move to Kent and said,

"It's not that, Len. It's just that this morning was the last time we would do things together. I suppose that strange countryside reminded me how far away you'll be in your new home. I don't know what it meant. I'm not sure it had to mean anything. Why do we see ghosts or dream weird things anyway? We've seen plenty of stranger and more frightening things over the last two or three years. I'm not going to worry about one more such experience," he lied. "I expect that after you move to Kent, we'll stop having paranormal visions, because that's all they are – just visions, Len. Nothing has ever hurt us."

"Yet," added Len.

Ann Compton had prepared a spread fit for a king – all the things that Len liked were there in the picnic party that, fortunately, quickly followed the two friend's discussion of otherworldly things. Reality returned to almost clear their minds of the morning's events, but Eddie would be haunted for some time by his special and personal meeting with the sixty-year-old version of his best friend. One final remark by Len's mum would also bring his other individual rendezvous with the elderly couple in the strange garden into added focus. It was just after six-thirty and Martha Wilby was helping Eddie's mum to clear away the aftermath of the picnic. Cyril Wilby was seated on the Compton's bench draining his third cup of tea – it had been a warm afternoon. Eddie had joined him for a chat about cars and Len's new school. Len had eaten too much and was visiting the toilet.

"What's Len's school like, Uncle Cyril?"

"It seems to be quite strict, Eddie. The Head is a strict disciplinarian."

"Len needs that, doesn't he?"

"Very observant of you, my boy. He won't get away with second best there. He'll have to work hard. You'll miss each other, won't you?"

"Yes. I hope he'll be alright."

"He'll be fine, Eddie."

'*Make sure you look after your family carefully*', echoed in Cyril Wilby's head. His wife broke his train of thought.

"Finished with your cup, dear?"

Eddie and Len didn't see each other again until the evening before the Wilbys were due to leave Fenton-on-Sea for good. Len had had too much to do during his last week and Eddie hadn't been able to face his friend again so soon after the doppelgänger at Linham Junction. He wanted to see Len desperately for one last time, particularly since he had bought him a small present as a token of their friendship. Fred Compton eventually persuaded his son to call round on Thursday the 29th.

"You must go and wish Len good luck, Eddie," he said just when it seemed that his son was going to disappear to his room to do some reading after his tea.

"Wish him well from us too," said Eddie's mum.

"Yes, Mum."

Eddie went upstairs to his bedroom and, pocketing Len's gift, he made his way to 7 Lime Tree Avenue for what would be the final time. Martha Wilby spotted Eddie before he had a chance to knock on the door. She was standing in the doorway as he walked up the front path.

"Hello, Eddie. I'm glad you've come. I've been trying to persuade Len all day to come and see you but he wouldn't."

Eddie smiled nervously as Len's mum ushered him into the bare hall. The house sounded hollow and echoey when Martha Wilby called upstairs,

"Eddie's here, Len. Come down."

A door opened and Len's voice echoed throughout the house.

"Tell him to come up, Mum."

Eddie climbed the stairs and went into his friend's bedroom. Len was sitting on his bed surrounded by boxes and other paraphernalia necessary for the following day's move. It all seemed so wrong to Eddie. Why did his best friend have to go? He was, after all, the friend that had been with him through all their incredible adventures – adventures that would have shocked the world if anyone knew. He was the friend that had looked after him since their junior school days and the friend that had kept the bullies away from him – those boys who were jealous or scared of his academic ability. He sat down beside his special friend and said chokingly,

"I've bought you a little present."

Eddie pulled the matchbox sized present from his pocket and placed it on the bed beside Len.

"Go on, open it," he said when his friend just stared at it.

"I didn't buy you anything, Eddie. I haven't had time, mate."

"Doesn't matter, Len. I'm not going anywhere – it's just something to send you on your way."

"Thanks, mate."

Len fumbled with the 'bon voyage' wrapping paper to reveal a small black box. He lifted the lid and gasped,

"Oh wow! It must have cost you a small fortune."

"Only a few weeks' pocket money. Put it on," said Eddie. "It will look after you wherever you go in the future."

Len's hands trembled as he lifted the solid silver St Christopher and chain. Eddie took the clasp and fastened it behind his friend's neck.

"He's the patron saint of travellers," said Eddie.

"I know. I've always wanted one."

He paused and then said,

"I'll never take it off; not even in the bath."

Eddie looked oddly at his friend's neck. The question that had bothered him all week still remained. Had the other 'Len' been wearing a chain? The white coat and close fitting tunic had hidden anything from view. Several times since the previous Saturday, Eddie had been on the point of taking the St Christopher back to the jeweller, but something stopped him on each occasion. He seemed to be caught up in some master plan for the future and it had frightened him. He couldn't tamper with the inevitable.

Eddie didn't stay long that evening. After a quick manly hug and a demand from Eddie that Len must write at least once a month, which he would reciprocate, the two boys parted. Familiar words were shouted and exchanged as Eddie walked down the Wilby's front path.

"See you, Captain Compton."

"Not if I see you first, comrade Len."

Both boys cried unashamedly as they went to sleep that night and both of them slept soundly undisturbed by dreams of phantoms and time travel.

6

Jenny Gets Some Advice

The weather matched Eddie's mood the following morning; it was grey, cool and damp. He wandered down the town at ten trying to avoid looking in the direction of Lime Tree Avenue. He also turned his head away from any red car or large lorry that passed him on South Road. Even the High Street seemed in sombre mood; few shoppers had so far braved the dank morning and most holidaymakers were still at their guest houses and B and Bs. Eddie ignored the shops and headed for the seafront. Len had told him previously that there was only sea between Fenton-on-Sea and the North Kent coast and that you could sail directly there. Standing on the promenade, Eddie stared out to sea at roughly forty-five degrees to his right and he immediately recalled a day in late May two years earlier. He and Len had 'flown' over that sea on their magic carpet at the beginning of their first fantastic adventure. Other thoughts came to him concerning Len and his family, especially after the previous day's party in his garden. He quickly gave a nervous shrug as if by so doing, he could banish them from his mind. It started to drizzle and Eddie walked back up the town, head down to avoid seeing removal lorries.

Unbeknown to Eddie, the Wilby's removal lorry didn't leave Fenton until just after eleven-thirty with the red Vauxhall Victor following. Cyril eventually overtook the lorry on the dualled part of the A132, arriving in Petersgate at three o'clock. Surprisingly, the lorry arrived only fifteen minutes later. By the time of the lorry's departure from Fenton, Eddie was already ensconced in his bedroom and reading a science fiction novel to cheer himself up with an escape into a fantasy world. He spent much of the remainder of the Friday in like manner – the weather did not improve.

Jenny Compton had the last day of July off from her job at Arleson's the bakers. She would normally work there on every other Saturday in the month. Her trainee fireman boyfriend, Gary, was spending the morning helping his dad at his second-hand car showroom in Hamsden. Jenny would take the eleven o'clock bus from South Road in order to meet him for lunch and shopping in the town afterwards. At breakfast Eddie announced that he wanted to go with her.

"But I've nothing to do now that Len's gone to Kent," he moaned at breakfast.

Jenny laughed.

"You are *not* going to play gooseberry. Go and find yourself a girlfriend or someone you can play trains with."

Jenny loved her brother dearly, but she still could not resist any opportunity to tease him mercilessly. She would probably do it for the rest of his life. Once an elder sister; always an elder sister – it went with the role.

"I don't play with trains anymore, sister dear."

"Yes, you do. Mum says you played with your toy train set only a few weeks ago outside on the lawn."

"That was different; *Len* wanted to do it one last time before he moved," lied Eddie. "I didn't enjoy it though."

'If only she knew', he thought. 'If only'.

"Well, Len's gone now, so get on with the rest of your life," said Jenny rather cruelly. Her mum interrupted the bickering.

"Stop it, Jennifer. Eddie is going to miss Len; they've been friends for such a long time. Just think what it would be like if Gary suddenly said he was going to pack up and leave you."

Eddie grinned at his sister. Jenny went quiet – she knew that it would be her worst nightmare.

"Sorry, Mum," and after an embarrassing pause she said, "Sorry, Eddie. I'll bring you something nice back from Hamsden."

The number 201 bus was fairly full when Jenny boarded it at the first stop in South Road. She managed to find an empty double seat on the top deck, so she wasn't squashed against any other passenger. Many people, holidaymakers included, had taken the opportunity provided by the wet weather to go shopping in the nearest large town. The beaches would be deserted for a change. Nobody else got on the bus right until it stopped unusually at the halt near the small village of Linham. Jenny's heart beat faster when she glanced at the field where the train crash had happened, and where her boyfriend had performed his heroics. She wanted to shout out and tell her fellow passengers of his deeds in saving some of the many injured from the burning wreck. Instead, she smiled with pride. He was *her* boyfriend and now he was going to be a fireman and a handsome one at that. The one extra passenger had climbed to the top deck and he stood nervously looking for a seat. Jenny spread herself across the two seats and looked nonchalantly out of the window, avoiding having to look at the new passenger. The passenger came down the aisle checking for empty seats. He stood by Jenny's seats.

"Excuse me, can I sit here?"

Jenny turned to face the voice and her mouth opened involuntarily. Standing over her was the most handsome young man she had ever seen. He was dressed in the most perfectly creased sailor's uniform. He was tall, muscular and had fair tousled hair. He looked to be about her age. She stammered,

"Yes, of-of course."

"Thanks."

Jenny quickly recovered her poise and, in her mind, she wondered why on earth a serving sailor would need to catch a bus at such an out-of-the-way place as Linham. She was too nervous to ask. He took out a cigarette case.

"Fancy a smoke?"

"No thanks. I don't."

"O.K. Mind if I do?"

"No, not at all."

"Thanks. It's been a long night."

Still Jenny daren't say anything. The sailor leant back in his seat and puffed smoke rings into the air. A couple of passengers opened some windows. Only one other person was smoking a pipe. The sailor closed his eyes. He seemed to be in a trance but was still able to tap the ash from his cigarette end at regular intervals until he finally stubbed it out as the bus approached the outskirts of Hamsden.

Ten minutes later the bus began to pull into the town's small bus station. The young sailor was the first to get up, clearly used to the jerky movement provided by the moving bus. He was about to walk up the aisle when he turned back and leant over Jenny. She could smell a mixture of after shave and tobacco smoke. It was not an unpleasant combination. He smiled and said,

"Take care, Jenny, and look after your brother over the next few weeks – he'll need your love."

Jenny froze in her seat and before she could say anything, the sailor had descended the stairs and had jumped from the still moving bus. She had a fleeting impression of something glinting around his neck.

Jenny was understandably subdued when she met up with her boyfriend. She had spent a few minutes searching the streets surrounding the bus station but the strange sailor had completely vanished. She decided against mentioning anything to Gary as he would only probably get the wrong idea. She would have found it difficult, in any case, to explain her total innocence in talking to the handsome young sailor. Gary was inordinately jealous of any of Jenny's casual admirers – and she had a few! Her mood, however, soon lightened after Gary had bought her lunch and treated her to a new leather handbag. It wouldn't be until much later that day that she would be reminded of her strange meeting on the bus.

Though Gary's driving ban – sustained as a result of his previous car crash – had been lifted, he had not yet bought another car and the young couple waited until Gary's father, Richard, had closed the showroom for the weekend. He gave them a lift back to Fenton in his Jaguar at a little after five-thirty. Jenny was in a good mood when she got back to Fir Tree Close. Eddie had just come downstairs from finishing his latest science fiction book when his sister came in through the front door.

"Look what Gary's bought me," she said triumphantly.

Eddie sneered.

"What do you want another bag for; you've got too many already."

"Three, if you must know, but this one is real leather," responded Jenny while she held the bag to her face and inhaled deeply. "Smell that," she continued, holding the bag out for Eddie to check.

"No thanks – I'd rather smell cigarette smoke. At least an animal hasn't been killed to make it."

Something that Eddie said – perhaps the mention of the word *cigarette* – caused Jenny to be reminded of the handsome young sailor. She ushered her brother upstairs before their parents were aware she was home.

"I've something to talk to you about, Eddie."

"What do you want?" he asked as she pushed and shoved him towards his bedroom.

"In private, brother."

Eddie sat on his bed while his sister remained standing by the window. This is important, he thought. What *could* she want?

"Eddie, I met someone today – on the bus to Hamsden this morning."

"So. Who?"

"A sailor."

"What's so special about that?"

"He knew me; he knew my name, Eddie."

"So. Plenty of people know you in Fenton-on-Sea; probably every boy or unattached man over the age of sixteen knows you, Jennifer Compton. You have a reputation. He probably used to go to Fenton Secondary Modern when you were there. How old was he?"

"About my age, nineteen or so – and, anyway, he wasn't from Fenton; I'm certain of that. He had his ship's name on his cap – HMS Connaught, I think."

"What did he want?" asked Eddie.

"He didn't want anything. He got on at Linham Junction and the only vacant seat was next to me. After he had sat down, he offered me a cigarette. But there's something else, Eddie."

The place name had sounded warning bells in Eddie's head before he asked,

"What?"

"He knew I had a brother."

"What did he look like?"

"He was tall, athletic and had fair hair."

Jenny omitted any description of his sexual appeal.

"How did he know me?" asked Eddie.

"He didn't say. He just told me…."

"Told you what?"

"That you would need looking after over the next few weeks and that you'd need my love."

Eddie grimaced.

"Did he remind you of anyone?"

"No, not really, but I think I may have heard his voice before. I just can't think where. His face may have been familiar, but…."

"But?"

"But his body wasn't. I'm sure I would have remembered seeing that before! Don't tell Mum about him, please, Eddie. She'll only worry or get the wrong idea. Promise?"

"I won't, I promise, Jenny."

"Good – I still can't think how he could know me or that I had a brother that might need looking after. I honestly think he has confused me with someone else."

"You mean there's another Jenny Compton in the area?" said Eddie with a smile. "I hope not, sister dear!"

"Well, I just don't know what to think; it's so weird that I'm beginning to think I must have dreamt the whole episode."

'If only you'd had the experiences that I'd had', thought Eddie, 'you'd think you were in a permanent dream!'

Jenny left her brother to his own thoughts. She didn't know that her 'weird' story had had more of an effect on him than she'd realised. For his part, Eddie hadn't dared question his sister about any silver jewellery that the young sailor might have been wearing. He didn't want Jenny to be aware that he might know his identity, if, indeed, it was the same person that he'd encountered on the strange road near the phantom nuclear power station. He wasn't about to share that piece of information with anyone, no matter how close they were. Even his best friend hadn't been told.

7
Letters

Exactly a week after Len had moved Eddie received a letter from his friend. He thought he recognised the handwriting on the envelope, and the Canterbury postmark confirmed his suspicions. He took it up to his bedroom to read; it seemed to contain several pages. He opened the envelope carefully and settled down to read. Len must have had help with the layout and spelling, he thought, but not, perhaps, with the punctuation.

23 The Park,
Petersgate,
Kent.
August 4th 1965

Dear Eddie,

Well here I am in sunny Kent. My bedroom is a bit bigger than the one I had in Fenton-on-Sea but at the moment I'm surrounded by boxes and piles of clothes. I don't have a wardrobe yet because the old one fell apart when we moved! The drive down last Friday was a bit scary as Dad doesn't really know the rule for overtaking on dual carriageways nor when to indicate when he turns corners. We hit eighty on the A2 and Mum screamed at him to slow down we stopped at a service area just after the Dartford Tunnel and after we returned from getting something to eat Dad couldn't get the car into reverse so we had to push until we could go forward which took ages.

Eddie giggled as he reread the sentence, thinking what Len's previous English teacher, Mr Green, would have said. He read on, fearing more punctuation howlers.

Petersgate is a bit bigger than Fenton but I don't think the beach is as nice because it always smells of rotting seaweed and boy does it stink. Dad says its good for the garden as a fertiliser. Have'nt made any friends yet there arnt any families with children in our road. Probably make some when I start school next month.

Again Eddie cringed at the several punctuation errors, but, at least he could understand what his friend had written. The letter continued.

What have you been doing? Are you going away on holiday anywhere? We're not, I think. Dad says we've got too much to do before we go back to school. Mum's got a part-time job at a paper shop in town – not quite like her old one as chief cook at Dad's old school but it's good money, she says. Dad nearly pranged the car when he picked her up yesterday. I think he should take his test again, but he doesn't listen to me. We get free newspapers as long as we wait until Mum comes home with them – she brought three yesterday. The local paper is called the Petersgate and Hargate Advertiser and it is full of adverts, much more than the Fenton Times.

Eddie guessed that someone had started to help him punctuate – the improvement was obvious for all to see.

Dad's trying to get tickets for Spurs first home game on August the 28th – they're playing local rivals Arsenal. Hope I can go and Eddie, you'll never guess what…

Eddie paused to say out loud,

"No I won't, Len. Go on surprise me."

… Tottenham are coming to Freeman Street for a pre-season friendly on the 17th. You must go – you'll see some real football when they thrash Hamsden Town seven or eight nil! I think it's an evening kick-off at 7.30. I wish I could go but Dad says it's just too far and we wouldn't get back until the early hours. Hope you can go and send me a report. Please get me a programme if they print any for the match. They may not as it's only a friendly.

Have you had anything strange happen to you since I left? I haven't. Well, Eddie, I can't think of anything else to write so I'll sign off now. Dad helped with some of this letter – you know I can't write for toffee. Anyway I've got to go and help him plant some conifers down one side of the back garden which is huge, Eddie; you should see it. Next door's fence doesn't give us enough privacy, Mum says. Goodbye, mate.

Best wishes,
Len

Eddie straightened out the three-page letter carefully and found an old book to keep it in. Before he did, however, he reread the final paragraph several more times. He himself had been in a long garden with conifers down one side, but they had been tall, he recalled – well over head height. The paranormal trip from his own garden had been brief, but Eddie was sure that the conifers had been in place for several years and that the garden's occupants had been old as well. A story was beginning to form his mind, but it was jumbled and consisted of seemingly unrelated events. However, which ever way he looked at it, they all led back to his best friend, Len. What did they signify? Were the events just random or was there a purpose too them? He felt certain that someone or something was trying to give him a message.

He decided he would buy a folder to store his friend's cards and letters in; he would try to keep them forever. He would write his reply later when he had decided what to put in it and, more importantly, what to leave out of it!

Jenny hadn't had any more strange liaisons that week and she had continued not to mention the one that she'd had to anyone else, especially her parents, who would only worry. Nevertheless, when she arrived home from work that Friday she was determined to ask them how Eddie was, particularly as it was only a week since his best friend had moved. She had an opportunity when he was slow in coming down from his bedroom for tea. Her mum didn't seem to be overly worried though.

"He's alright, I think, dear; he just spends a lot of time by himself, but that's to be expected – Len's not here," she said somewhat obviously. "He was cheered up when he received a nice long letter from him this morning."

"I just wondered if he was O.K. physically, Mum. I know he's always been mentally disturbed!"

Fred Compton looked over the top of his newspaper.

"Physically? What on earth do you mean, Jenny? He's a healthy fourteen-year-old lad with all that entails. He's at the crossroads before he reaches manhood proper. Give him time and he'll turn out fine."

"I just thought he looked a little odd the other day, but I suppose you're right, Mum – he's missing Len."

"What do you mean – odd?" asked Jenny's mum.

"Kind of vague; as though he was somewhere else in his own little world."

Fred Compton grinned.

"Well you know your brother as well as anybody, Jenny. He's always seemed to be in his own world. He reads too many science fiction books, if you ask me."

"Better than reading railway timetables, Dad," said Jenny.

Eddie was standing in the doorway. Jenny looked sheepish. How long had her brother been there? She threw out a feeler.

"Hello, brother dear. We were just talking about you."

"Were you, sister dear? What's better than reading railway timetables?"

Jenny was visibly relieved. Her brother had only caught the very tail end of the conversation. Ann Compton said,

"Reading science fiction, dear. Your dad thinks you read too much of it."

"Does he? Well at least I *can* read, Mum – unlike my sister here who only buys magazines to look at the pictures."

'Well, thanks', thought Jenny. 'So much for sticking up for you and being concerned for your well-being. Thanks a lot, brother'.

Len was first to the post the following day; he had hoped that there would be a return letter from Eddie, even though he had only posted his own on the Wednesday. He wanted to hear his friend's news – he had a feeling that Eddie was missing him more than he'd realised. There was one letter for his dad; only a few people had their new address yet. He was clearly disappointed when he handed over the letter from South Eastern Gas.

"What's up, son?"

"Nothing much, Dad – I was just hoping that Eddie would have sent me a letter. I've sent him one."

"When did you send it?"

"Wednesday morning."

"Well that would be a bit quick to get one back in three days. This letter is postmarked Thursday and it's taken two days from Canterbury, seven miles away. I expect you'll get a reply by Monday or Tuesday."

"I suppose so," said Len finally.

On the surface, Len would never admit to having many emotional feelings. He had been very brave in accepting his parents' move but deep down, like Eddie, he was missing his best friend. He just didn't show it. His dad interrupted his thoughts.

"What are you going to do today? Your mum and I are going to do some more unpacking, but you don't need to stay in and help. It looks like a nice day outside. Why don't you do some exploring; go to Canterbury on the bus or something."

Len began to cheer up. His dad's suggestion sounded like a good idea and he had some saved money to spend too. The Wilbys weren't taking a holiday that summer and extra pocket money had been provided by way of consolation.

It turned out to be quite a long walk to the nearest bus stop from the leafy avenues of Petersgate where The Park was located. It was three-quarters of a mile to the Canterbury road where Len had a choice of stops which were a few hundred yards in either direction – left into town or right to the outskirts. He chose right and only just made the stop as a red and blue double-decker of the East Kent Roadcar Company lumbered up behind him. Climbing aboard, he made his way to the upper deck. The bus was full with Saturday morning shoppers and there was just one seat available next to an elderly and rather scruffily dressed man. The man clearly had hygiene problems and Len felt uncomfortable in the warm and stuffy atmosphere. He tried to breathe shallowly. The man seemed to be asleep.

Part of the journey took Len down the A2 in the direction of the East Kent coast which was jammed with holidaymakers heading for the beaches at Margate and Ramsgate. The bus slowed to a crawl. Sensing the change in the sound of the big diesel engine, the old man woke up. Len leant away to the aisle. The bus suddenly turned right, throwing Len back against the old man.

"Sorry, sir," he said politely.

The old man grunted. Len looked into the man's face for the first time. Len recognised the stranger immediately – it was the tramp who had saved him and Eddie the previous summer in Devon. It was Jacob Manders! Len was bold.

"Hello, Mr Manders. It's Len – Len Wilby."

The old man seemed not to have heard Len's greeting. A woman passenger directly behind Len must have heard what he'd said.

"He's deaf, dear. He can't hear you."

Len turned round to address the lady who had spoken.

"But I know him."

"Everybody knows old Bill. He used to be a policeman in Dover until he lost his hearing. That's why we call him 'Old Bill'. The name fits, doesn't it?"

'Bill' had gone back to sleep and Len turned back to look more closely at his face. He couldn't believe how he had made such a stupid mistake. The man looked nothing like the ghostly Mr Manders. His mind was playing tricks or….

The number 4A pulled into Canterbury bus station at ten-thirty and Len made to leave his seat, squeezing into the line of passengers all eagerly trying to get to the lower deck. A voice whispered from behind him.

"Be careful, Len. Be very careful."

Len turned round. 'Old Bill' still seemed sound asleep. All the other passengers were busily chatting to each other. Before he had time to investigate further, he was jostled forward and almost fell down the stairs and out into the warm morning sunshine. Len waited. A few minutes later and the conductor escorted 'Old Bill' down from the top deck and saw him safely on his way. The deaf old man shuffled across the road and was soon lost in the Saturday morning crowds. Len didn't follow. He didn't need to. The voice surely hadn't belonged to the old man or, indeed, Jacob Manders. It had been his best friend's voice.

One hundred and fifty miles north of Canterbury, the weather in Fenton-on-Sea had turned wet and windy. As Len was gazing in awe at the splendour of England's finest cathedral, Eddie made the decision to write a reply to his friend's letter. There was not much else he could do that morning. He sat at the makeshift desk in his bedroom and tried to think of what to say. It took him ten minutes and three wasted pieces of his mum's good writing paper before he found a way of starting the letter.

38 Fir Tree Close,
Fenton-on-Sea,
Suffolk,
Saturday a. m.

Dear Len,

Thank you very much for your letter and all your news. It's pouring down outside so I'm stuck inside. Jenny and Dad are both at work while Mum has just popped next door to see Aunty Beth.

Not much has happened since you left except that my sister says she met a young sailor on the bus to Hamsden. I think she fancied him. She says that the sailor knew her name and also that she had a brother.

I've never met any sailors in Fenton, have you? I'm convinced she made the whole thing up, but it did worry me for a while as she said he got on the bus at Linham Junction. Maybe my sister's seeing ghosts now. Maybe it was a friend of old Granty or the bloke in the white coat at the phantom power station, Len!

Eddie sat back in his chair and put his best fountain pen down. He had got through the worst bit – he didn't need to say who he'd thought the young sailor was, let alone the scientist in the white coat. He also didn't need to suggest that they might have been the same person. He got down to more mundane issues.

I've read two new science fiction books since you left and I now have a library ticket which means I can take out up to four books at a time. I was going to Hamsden on the train today but I'll have to go next week as it's still raining hard, just ready for the football season which starts in two weeks. Mum and Dad say I can go to see the Town whenever I want and on my own, now I'm fourteen, except if it's midweek and in term time. I will definitely go Tuesday week and watch Tottenham play. Dad says that Town are a good bet for promotion to the Second Division this year – we've just signed the Irish international, Johnny McBride for £40,000, our most expensive ever purchase. But still nothing like how much Tottenham spend on a player. I hope you won't be too upset when Hamsden beat you on the 17th!

It's carnival week coming up and the shops are taking part in the 'Window Competition' as usual. This year you have to find an object that doesn't belong in the shop; something they wouldn't sell. There are fifty-three altogether, so it'll keep me busy until I get bored. Does Petersgate have a carnival? Do they have a football team? Dad says they might be in the Southern League.

My sister finishes at Arleson's in two weeks. She's been there since she was sixteen. She's off to Hamsden Civic College in September to start a Beauty Therapy and Hairdressing course – hope there's not a written exam. Dad had to help her fill out the application form, but I suppose Gary loves her.

One last thing, Len – Dad's going to buy a new car. Our Morris Minor is falling to pieces; we've had it for ten years. I want him to get a Jaguar, but Dad says they're too expensive. I think he might go for something like your dad's – I know he was a bit jealous when you got it. Hope your dad's driving is improving! Can your mum drive? My mum is going to take lessons soon. Dad had refused to teach her! Says she's too nervous to drive.

Well, no more for now. I will send you a programme from the match on the 17th. Take care of yourself. You never know I may see you soon.

Your best friend

Eddie

PS Send me some photos of your new house and Petersgate.

Eddie carefully folded the four small sheets of blue Basildon Bond writing paper and inserted them into the matching envelope. He stuck the fourpenny stamp in the top right hand corner and addressed the front of the envelope. Condensing all his thoughts and worries into the letter had been quite emotional and, at times, he had found it difficult to know what to say. He thought he had done a pretty good job, omitting, of course, the possible sighting of his best friend's ghost.

He decided to finish the task there and then by taking the letter directly to the main post office in the High Street. The rain had eased slightly when he left the house and it wasn't an unpleasant experience to walk in the steady refreshing drizzle. It helped him to clear away any worrying and ghostly thoughts from his mind.

8

The Spurs Come to Town

Len got lost a couple of times as he wandered round the maze of back streets in Canterbury. He occasionally caught glimpses of the deaf man, but he didn't approach him. Eddie's voice had seemed to come out of thin air – it hadn't come from 'Old Bill's' mouth, he thought; he had been fast asleep when Len had turned round. Len was troubled but eventually put the experience down to the oppressive atmosphere on the bus making him feel giddy and sleepy. The familiar voice had been entirely within his head, he decided.

He spent an hour or two browsing in the city's many bookshops, both modern and antiquarian in nature, but found nothing to interest him. A large bag of chips and a bottle of orangeade sated his hunger and thirst and by two o'clock he found himself back at the entrance to the cathedral. He hadn't gone inside when he'd first arrived that morning but the day was now becoming unbearably hot, so he sought sanctuary in the shade and the coolness within. He found a seat near the altar to rest and take in the atmosphere. The cathedral was crowded with visitors of many different nationalities. He sensed a presence behind him. It was enhanced by a familiar smell. He turned round. It was 'Old Bill'. He nodded at Len who stared back in silence. Despite the old man's advancing years, his face looked somehow strangely familiar. He began to speak quietly.

"Spare a few coppers for an old soldier, comrade."

His voice echoed in Len's head.

"Ye-yes, sir," said Len.

'Old Bill' quickly pocketed the bright new sixpence that Len gave him. He got to his feet and shuffled away down the main aisle. Len was

81

too stunned to follow. Only one other person had ever called him 'comrade'.

Eventually, Len managed to shake himself together and he made for the main entrance as quick as he dared without causing a scene. He was too late – Eddie's 'ghost' was nowhere to be seen. He sat down on some stone steps and put his head in his hands. He had to think. Unlike before, this time he was convinced that the old man had spoken with his best friend's voice. Could two people, who differed in age by over fifty years, have the same sounding voice? Was he just hearing things because he was missing Eddie and he wanted to hear his voice? Was it the heat of the day? Was 'Old Bill' how his friend would be in fifty or more years time? If this was true, then why, on the bus, did he warn Len to *'be careful, very careful'*? Was he in some sort of danger? All these questions kept stabbing at his brain like arrows.

He was lost in his own world for many minutes as he sat in the warm afternoon sunshine. He ignored the several passers-by who brushed past him in his position in the middle of the small square in front of the cathedral gates. He looked at his watch. It was ten to four. Where had the time gone? He'd been at the cathedral for nearly two hours. He stood up on stiff legs and began to make his way back to the bus station. Though he was troubled by the meetings with the old man, he wasn't as scared as he would have been had he known that his best friend's sister had had a similar meeting with a young sailor who'd also conveyed a message to her. He caught the number 4 bus for the return journey to Petersgate and fortunately, by the time he walked into 23 The Park, he had put the stranger events of the day to the back of his mind. He'd had enough of trying to work out what it all might mean.

The Fenton-on-Sea carnival turned out to be a virtual wash-out as the rain poured down all day on Saturday the 14th. Eddie didn't go and watch; neither did he win the 'Window Competition'. Neither boy experienced anything else exceptional and by the morning of the day of the pre-season friendly with Spurs, Eddie's mind was only focused on that evening's game. Because the evenings were still light until after nine, he had been allowed to take the train to Hamsden; it was the best way because Freeman Street was less than half a mile from the railway station.

Catching the ten past six train from Fenton, Eddie arrived at the ground at five to seven and was surprised how few people there seemed to be about. Had he got the wrong day? He had checked the local paper carefully, he thought. Town's usual Saturday gates were about 8,000, but when he had paid his three shillings and was stood in the North stand, he calculated that there were less than a few hundred inside the ground. He was able to get right down to the front – just a few feet from the touchline. By twenty past seven the crowd had only swelled to a thousand or so; the stadium looked empty and sounded hollow when any chanting started from the terraces. Eddie spotted a fellow grammar school pupil standing a few yards away. He was in the year above Eddie and Eddie only knew him vaguely. Eddie approached him tentatively and said,

"There are not many people here, are there?"

The older boy knew Eddie and surprised him when he addressed him by name.

"No, Mr Compton, there aren't. Apparently Tottenham are only sending their reserve team – it was on the radio earlier."

"Oh," said Eddie. "That's a shame. I was hoping to see Greavesy play."

"There won't be anybody we've heard of," said the older boy who then introduced himself as one Danny Chambers. Eddie mumbled something in reply as Danny moved away to be some friends who'd just arrived. Eddie was cross. It was typical of the big London club not to send their first team. Hamsden Town F.C. of the Third Division was obviously not good enough to warrant a visit from their superstars. 'Still', Eddie thought, 'if we win, it will still be a victory against the mighty Spurs'. He opened his sixpenny programme and looked at the team sheets in the centre. At the top it read:

Hamsden Town F.C. v Tottenham Hotspur Reserves

It wasn't the mighty Spurs, just their second team. It didn't count. He didn't study their list of players. Town seemed to be at full strength with Johnny McBride at centre forward. Five minutes later and the visitors, mostly consisting of players in their teens or early twenties, took the field to a mixture of jeers and polite applause. A chorus of '*Come on the Town*' echoed round the nearly empty ground to greet the home side a minute later. Eddie moved to a position behind the north end goal; a lone cameraman sat on the grass in front of him.

Hamsden Town kicked off with their goalkeeper, Bob Dean, occupying the goal at Eddie's end. The first twenty minutes were interrupted continually by the over zealous referee until Tottenham scored a lucky deflected goal. Minutes later and the Spurs' fair-haired inside right headed just wide. The ball bounced on the retaining wall in front of Eddie and straight into his waiting arms. He caught it cleanly and was just about to throw it back when the momentum of the young reserve forward sent him almost crashing into the wall in front of Eddie.

"Give us the ball, mate," said the young footballer.

Eddie lobbed the ball into the young player's arms. He smiled knowingly and said,

"Thanks, Captain."

The tall fair-haired footballer winked and trotted back up the field.

Though his neck was bare, Eddie thought he'd guessed the identity of the inside right without the extra confirmation provided by a quick glance at the Tottenham team sheet. With eyes that struggled to focus, he read who Tottenham's number eight was. He *saw* L. Wilby. He closed the programme quickly. It was impossible, just impossible. This was unreal. This was a totally new twist in ghostly liaisons. Previously, the ghosts, whether of his friend or not, had not been real and they had disappeared afterwards. This one was his best friend, Len, aged about nineteen and his name was written down for all to see! It just couldn't be. He couldn't concentrate on the game for the rest of the first half and avoided looking at the opposition's number eight in particular. The half-time whistle blew. The players left the field with the score still 1-0 to the visiting team. Eddie looked at the programme again. He couldn't believe how stupid he'd been. He was beginning to see his best friend everywhere. Anyone tall and fair-haired seemed to fit the bill. The name on the opposition's team sheet actually read L. Wilton – a simple mistake? Eddie wasn't sure. Had his mind played a trick on him by letter or word association, especially when the young footballer had called him 'Captain'? He had to get to grips with himself or he might start seeing ghosts at every turn. He had been convinced that he had seen Len at the power station but the incident with the young footballer began to sow the seeds of doubt in his mind. If he could misread a team sheet he could misread a lapel badge. It had happened in a flash. However, it would not be long before Eddie would realise that he *hadn't* made a mistake at Linham Junction and also that a greater power was deliberately setting reminders in his path. His mind was not his own.

The second half proved to be disastrous for Hamsden Town. They eventually conceded three more goals with only a last minute penalty as a consolation. 4–1 wasn't a true reflection of the game and Town's defence would need to tighten up before the start of the season proper on the coming Saturday. Eddie didn't see the Leonard look-a-like up close again; he stayed permanently in or around Town's penalty area at the opposite end to where Eddie continued to stand. From a distance he couldn't understand how he had mistaken the young player for an older version of his friend.

On the train home Eddie sat behind Danny Chambers and his friends and he listened while Danny spouted off about how weak Town's defence had been.

"Old Fred Phillips was awful; he let that young inside forward run rings round him."

Danny turned round to Eddie and said,

"You did well to catch his header, Compton. I remember you saving a penalty in the Under 13's cup final. Are you in the Under 15's next year?"

"No, I was only a late replacement when the first choice keeper went down with flu in the epidemic. I haven't played football for the school since."

"Pity – you still seem to have the same anticipation. I'll never know how you guessed which way to go when you saved the penalty."

Eddie smiled as he remembered Len's 'magic' football. Just another episode from the fantasy world he and Len had occupied at times. Danny returned to his conversation with his friends while Eddie gazed out of the train window at the darkening sky. It had been an interesting evening.

The following evening, Eddie's dad brought a copy of the Hamsden Daily Star home from work for his son to read the report of the match. He presented it to Eddie with great ceremony at teatime.

"You'd better look at the back page, son. There's something that might interest you."

The back page had a photograph of a young fair-headed Tottenham footballer heading narrowly past a goal post. In the bottom right-hand corner stood a startled teenage boy catching the ball in both arms. Eddie remembered the cameraman; he must have moved quickly to one side when he saw L. Wilton leap skywards. Eddie's mum was full of pride for her son.

"I must get the original photograph, Fred. We'll have it framed. You never know but the young Spurs player might become famous one day – even an international. You just never know. He's certainly handsome."

Ann Compton continued to stare proudly at the photograph and her next words started Eddie worrying again.

"He looks a lot like Len, Eddie – or, at least, how Len could look in a few years time."

'So', thought Eddie, 'anyone can make the same mistake. He did look like Len'.

Later in his room, he would look at his programme again, double and treble-checking the name of the Tottenham reserve number eight. Each time it would still read L. Wilton. Nevertheless, it would continue to bother and nag Eddie for some time – the name was just too close to his friend's for it to be a coincidence. His mum thought he had looked like Len too. As he lay in bed that night, a question came to add another twist to his thoughts. 'Could ghosts come back as different people? Were L. Wilton and L. Wilby one and the same person? But that would mean that

Len was already....' Eddie dismissed the thought that was forming in his mind and went to sleep. That was stupid!

9

A Reunion on the Beach

On the Saturday following Eddie's first visit to Freeman Street, Hamsden Town provided the large holiday crowd of nearly 11,000 with a superb victory over Bestcott Rovers from England's second city, Birmingham. Two goals from Johnny McBride and two penalties struck home by their captain 'Woody' Bates saw Town to a comfortable 4–0 scoreline. Eddie was ecstatic after he had returned home on the train. At teatime he couldn't stop talking about the new Irish striker.

"He's brilliant, Dad. You should have seen his second goal. He must have hit it from forty yards. I wish Len could have been with me," he said wistfully.

"I expect he's gone to White Hart Lane, son," said Eddie's dad.

"I don't think so, Dad. Len said in his letter that Spurs' first home game was on the 28th; that's next Saturday. His dad was trying to get tickets."

"You'll have to write and tell him about the game," said Ann Compton.

"I will, Mum, but it's Len's turn to write. I wrote yesterday to tell him about Tuesday's game and I sent him the programme as well. We're going to send letters once a month, if we can. I'm keeping his letters in a folder."

"Did you tell him about your photograph being in the paper and that the Spurs striker looked a bit like him? That would cheer him up."

"I just told him about the photo, Mum."

Eddie's mum smiled and said,

"Wouldn't it be good if Len becomes a star footballer one day? You would be able to say that you played with him when you were boys."

"I don't think he's that good, Mum – he never made the county team when he was at Fenton Grammar."

Sunday turned out to be a scorching hot day with temperatures already in the eighties by the time Eddie's mum and dad left as usual for morning service at St Andrew's overlooking the seafront. It had been some years since Eddie's sister had accompanied them but just a few short weeks since her brother had joined her in protesting the point of such regular and monotonous attendance. Eddie's burgeoning interest in science and its opinion as to the origin of the universe had dampened his belief in God. That belief, however, had not been eradicated completely. Indeed, recent events had halted its slow deterioration. Eddie did believe there was a greater power at work in the world, or, at least, *his* world. He wasn't as yet aware, however, how much it was also impinging on his best friend's world.

After his parents had left to attend church and with Jenny still in bed, Eddie decided to take a good long walk along the Fenton's two-mile promenade. He would start in the middle at the foot of Steep Hill, go north to the end at Mason's Point and then retrace his steps to walk the promenade's full length to its other extremity, South End, before returning to his starting point. In all it would be a distance of at least five miles. It would give him time to think and, hopefully, put things into context and reality. He would let his scientific mind dominate and sort his worries out.

The promenade seemed strangely quiet as Eddie turned left and headed towards Mason's Point. Above, clouds had swept in off the sea and it had turned noticeably cooler. Eddie found it more comfortable than the walk down the High Street. He strode out with some vigour and determination. Looking up ahead, Eddie couldn't see another person between himself and the Point. 'Where is everybody?' he thought. There had been a fair few families heading for the beach when he had walked down the High Street. It was much cooler now and it seemed to Eddie that it was much earlier than he had thought. But he hadn't left home until after ten-thirty, he was sure of that. Mum and Dad had already gone to church by then. He looked east and out to sea. The clouds parted to reveal the sun lower in the sky than when it had last been exposed. 'Oh no', he thought. 'It's happening again'. He'd moved time. There were signs, however, that it was still summer: a deckchair attendant removing a tarpaulin; remains of ice creams and drink bottles on the beach. It was early morning. Eddie approached the attendant.

"Have you got the time, please?"

"Yes, lad – it's just gone half past eight."

Eddie thanked the man and moved on. The sea was right out; it had been high tide when he'd arrived on the promenade. He decided to walk on the damp sand by the water's edge. It gave him a better view of the seafront. All seemed normal. One or two beach huts and guest houses had had a fresh lick of paint, but there was nothing much else to tell Eddie that he had moved very far into the future or the past. He thought he knew the deckchair man by sight but he hadn't appeared greatly older or younger. Eddie walked on. After another fifty yards or so he spotted someone else coming towards him in the distance. Eddie strained his eyes and could just make out that the figure was a boy of about his own age but, perhaps, slightly taller. The boy approached. He had fair hair. Eddie nodded knowingly to himself. It had to be Len. The boy got to within ten feet. It was Len but, yet, it wasn't Len. This boy was taller, slightly broader and seemed older, about fifteen or sixteen. 'Len' spoke.

"What'cha, Eddie."

Eddie stammered his reply – he hadn't got used to talking to ghosts.

"Oh hello, Len – what on earth are you doing here, mate?"

"We've just come back for a few days. How've you been?"

"You didn't say in your letter that you were coming back."

Len smiled but didn't reply. He turned to walk in the same direction as Eddie whose head was spinning in disbelief. Here was a marginally older version of his best friend and this time it was definitely him, no question. Should he give him a hug or shake his hand? He decided against it for fear of there being nothing there to hug or shake. Should he tell him that he was a ghost come back to haunt him? Len sensed his friend's dilemma and changed the conversation to his own world.

"Did you see the final yesterday? What a fantastic result for our boys!"

Now Eddie was really lost and confused, but he had to ask the obvious question from his world.

"What final?"

"The World Cup Final, you idiot! We won 4–2; Geoff Hurst scored a hat-trick. You must have seen it."

It was Eddie's turn to remain silent. What could he say? However, he thought he knew which year he'd moved to. Len was definitely older and the next World Cup was scheduled for the following year so it had to be 1966 (Len didn't look five years older, that would make him twenty).

The two boys walked on in silence. All sorts of questions were going through Eddie's mind. Did Len know he was a ghost? On the other hand, if Len was real and in his own world of 1966, then did he think that Eddie was a ghost from the past? Had he glimpsed the future? Would Len and his family come back to Fenton-on-Sea next summer? One frightening question eventually cleared the other more philosophical ones away. Could he get back to August the 22nd, 1965 or was he stuck with his friend about a year in the future?

They reached the line of boulders that formed the sea defences at Mason's Point. The two boys had walked a quarter of a mile in absolute silence with Eddie, for one, longing to reach out and touch his best friend; longing to tell him that it was 1965 and that he'd only just moved from Fenton and, above all, longing to talk to him about what it all meant, like they always used to. Len, however, broke the silence first.

"Got to go, mate – our guest house is over there. May see you later."

Before Eddie had a chance to reply, 'Len' bounded up the beach towards the promenade. Eddie's last sight of his best friend was his bobbing head as he reached the road on the far side. He ran up the beach as quickly as the soft sand would allow but there was no sign of Len's ghost when Eddie reached the road. He somehow knew there wouldn't be – there were no guest houses within half a mile of that stretch of the seafront.

It had turned suddenly hotter again and, as Eddie turned round to look at the beach, the sun was once again high in the sky. The prom was filling up with holidaymakers out for a lunchtime stroll. Eddie breathed a sigh of relief. He had returned to 1965.

Eddie was too excited and on edge to complete his intended walk and he made his way back to Steep Hill via the Undercliff. He tried hard to remember what Len had said in their short and ghostly conversation but nothing would come back apart from the year – 1966. Bookmakers up and down the land would breathe a sigh of relief that some greater power had wiped Edward Compton's memory clear of any facts about future World Cup Final results!

Though Len had been slightly older, there had been something else different about him that Eddie couldn't quite put his finger on until he reached the top of Steep Hill and entered the High Street. He was deep in thought as he wandered past Neville's the jeweller, the shop where he'd bought.... All sorts of rings and necklaces glinted at him in the bright sunshine and instantly he remembered. Len hadn't been wearing his St Christopher. Eddie stared at his own reflection in the shop window. Len's neck had been bare; his simple white T-shirt hadn't hidden a thing. He'd promised Eddie he would never take it off. A few moments passed and eventually Eddie shrugged his shoulders and continued on his walk home. Len had been a ghost and ghosts could wear what they liked. Len's other ghost, the scientist at the nuclear power station, *might* have been wearing the medallion anyway. Jenny hadn't told her brother that the young sailor *had* been wearing a necklace of some kind and Eddie continued to think about the St Christopher for the rest of the walk home. He was late as a glance at the station clock revealed. It was gone half past one and Sunday lunch would be on the table.

Sunday lunch wasn't on the table when Eddie arrived home. In fact the Comptons wouldn't eat the wasted meal that day. Eddie's mum was waiting in the doorway to 38 Fir Tree Close when her son reached the front gate. She wasn't smiling. Eddie called up the front path,

"Sorry I'm late, Mum – forgot the time."

Ann Compton didn't reply and her strained facial expression didn't change. She walked forward and held her son in her arms. Eddie protested.

"Mum, stop it!"

Eddie's mum started to cry and Eddie could feel her body trembling. He knew something serious was wrong. He extricated himself from her hug and stood back to face her. They were now standing just inside the front door.

"What's the matter, Mum? What's happened?"

Eddie's dad was standing almost helplessly behind his wife in the hall and said,

"Get him into the lounge, love."

Eddie looked at his dad's face and said,

"Please tell me what's happened, Dad?"

Fred Compton ushered and cajoled his son into the lounge and pointed to a chair.

"Sit down, son. We've got some bad news to tell you."

Eddie looked round the lounge. His mum had remained in the hall.

"Where's Jenny, Dad?" croaked Eddie. "It's Jen, isn't it? Something's happened to Jenny."

"No, son – it's not Jenny. She's in her bedroom."

"Then, who...?"

"It's Len, Eddie."

Eddie heard his mum sob in the background.

"Len?"

"Look, son, there's no easy way for us to tell you this, I'm afraid."

What Eddie's dad said next didn't immediately seem to register in Eddie's head and he said,

"But I've just...."

As soon as he'd uttered these words, few though they were, he realised how, at the same time, they were both pointed and pointless.

10

Tragedy

Len and his dad had decided to get up very early on Sunday, August the 22nd – fishing off the pier at Deal was the order of the day. They set off just after eight on a beautiful sunny morning with a fresh, autumnal feel to the air. The journey via the A2 to Ramsgate would take about forty-five minutes. Cyril Wilby had checked the local tables and high tide was scheduled to be at nine-fifteen – the best time for mackerel and bass, he told his son.

Len's dad pulled the red Vauxhall Victor onto the A2 at the Queen's roundabout intersection and he opened the throttle as they headed east. He soon had the big car up to its cruising speed of seventy miles per hour. They crested the brow of a small hill and saw the East Kent coast spread out before them. The car's engine was purring and it seemed to Cyril that it deserved to be put to the test. He depressed the accelerator further and said,

"Let's see what she'll do, son."

"Oh yes, Dad. Give her all she's got. We can see for miles."

The road in front pointed like an arrow into the distance. There was nothing else on the road. The car sped on towards the horizon.

"What are we doing now, Dad," said Len excitedly.

His dad began counting out loud.

"Eighty-five, eighty-six, eighty-seven...."

The engine whined but was not protesting. They touched ninety. Three ravens and a magpie scattered into a field to the left of the car's speeding progress; a pigeon ignored the red tornado and was nearly crushed by the front wheels. Len looked back.

"Missed it, Dad – would have been twenty points!"

Len's dad grunted.

"I'll get him on the way back."

But he wouldn't be going back that way later that day. A roundabout signified the eastern end of the A2. It was still six hundred yards ahead. Cyril Wilby kept his foot down. He had never driven a vehicle at this speed; he had never had to judge when and how fast to brake. Army vehicles rarely went faster than fifty and the red Vauxhall was doing more than ninety. A large sign to the left gave the first warning to slow down and another followed almost instantly. Len shouted the obvious.

"Slow down, Dad. There's a roundabout!"

Len's dad hit the brake and the big car shuddered and weaved first left and then right as its driver fought to keep it in a straight line. They were less than a hundred yards from the walled roundabout. Len shouted again and braced himself.

"We're not going to make it!"

Beads of perspiration exuded from his dad's forehead as he gripped the wheel like a madman. If anyone had been following they would have seen a huge cloud of smoke pour from the screaming back wheels. Neither of them had a chance to say or even think anything more. The car hit the four foot concrete banking that surrounded the roundabout. If measured, the impact speed would have been recorded in excess of fifty-five. The engine compartment was crushed to a fraction of its size. The steering column buried itself in Cyril Wilby's chest. He felt no pain as he died instantly. Len was knocked unconscious as his head hit the windscreen. Thankfully, he too felt no pain as his mangled lifeless body was launched over the walled surround and almost to the other side of the roundabout. His bright silver St Christopher was torn off in the crash and landed a few feet away to his left. It would be found on the Monday by accident investigators who would eventually return it to Cyril Wilby's widow. Martha would just have time to replace it round her dead son's neck before his coffin was closed for the last time just before the funeral. It was just after eight-thirty. After a couple of minutes, the first of several cars stopped and the driver would be able to tell the police later the approximate time of the tragic accident. On a beach a hundred and fifty miles away, another fourteen-year-old boy had just asked a deckchair attendant for the time.

Before Eddie had received his tragic news that Sunday afternoon, Ann and Fred Compton had been home from church for just over an hour. The Reverend Henry Weaver had delivered his usual thought provoking sermon; friendship and earthly love had been his themes. As a consequence, Eddie's mum had decided to phone her friend Martha in Kent; Fred Compton was happy that the weekend call would be at the cheapest rate. He knew how long his wife could talk to her best friend. It was ten to one. A strange voice answered.

"Hello, can I help you?"

"Oh yes, can I speak to Martha, please?"

Silence. Ann thought she detected someone talking in the background. The pause seemed to last for ages. The voice came back.

"I'm sorry; she's unable to come to the phone right now."

"Oh," said Ann Compton, "will you tell her it's Ann from Fenton-on-Sea; I'm her best friend."

More discussion off-phone. Ann thought she could hear crying. What was wrong? She heard the telephone change hands to be followed by someone sobbing into it.

"Martha? Is that you? What ever is the matter?" asked Eddie's mum quietly.

"Ann, oh Ann," said Martha Wilby between sobs.

"What? What is it?"

Ann knew something serious had happened, despite her friend's tendency to exaggerate crises at times. The emotions she was hearing suggested a real tragedy of some kind. The line went silent for a few moments.

"Martha? Are you still there, dear?"

"I'm here," came the quavering reply. It was clear Martha couldn't go on.

She said simply,

"I can't talk now."

The phone was passed back to the voice.

"I'm sorry but Ann's had some bad news. I'm her neighbour, Sue Rogers. She wants me to tell you."

"What? What's happened?"

It's her husband and son; they've been tragically killed in a road accident. I'm so sorry. It happened earlier this morning at just after half past eight."

Ann Compton couldn't say anything and Sue Rogers continued.

"She's in good hands; some relations are on their way from Cambridge and a couple of us neighbours are staying with her till then. I believe it's her sister and husband who are coming down."

Martha had never talked to Ann about her family. She knew that her parents were both dead. Ann always felt like family – the two women were like sisters. She plucked up courage and said,

"We'll come down as soon as we can. Would you give Martha our sincere condolences and tell her we're thinking of her and that we love her dearly."

"I will; of course I will."

Ann couldn't manage the pleasantries of some parting words and put the phone down. She stood in the hall and cried uncontrollably.

There was, of course, nothing that the emergency services could do in the aftermath of the accident other than dampen down the smouldering wreck of Cyril's prized Vauxhall Victor. Identification would take place at a suitable and appropriate time. For the time being the next of kin had to be informed, details of whom were found from a diary that Cyril Wilby always carried. Two police officers and a young woman bereavement counsellor, provided by the service, broke the tragic news to Martha at about eleven o'clock at her new home in The Park at Petersgate. Martha didn't cry immediately and the counsellor knew that the shock often delayed any public outpouring of grief till later. Martha spent half an hour in complete silence. She alternated from sitting in a chair staring at a picture of her late husband and standing gazing out of the lounge window at her newly planted and rearranged garden. By the time her new neighbour, Mrs Sue Rogers, had arrived at the request of the police counsellor, she was ready to let her emotions take over and she cried freely into the arms of a virtual stranger. Sue held Martha for a good ten minutes until the first of many such natural and essential outpourings subsided, brought about only by the telephone ringing in the hall. It was ten to one and it was nearly two hours since Martha had received her tragic news.

Eddie's mum wanted to jump straight into the car and head for Kent, but her husband knew that too many visitors for Martha too soon would not be a good thing and Ann was persuaded to wait until at least the following day. On hearing the news, Eddie had disappeared immediately to his bedroom. He had not said another word to his parents after the initial attempt to tell them that he had just seen his best friend on Fenton beach. He spent most of the afternoon reading and rereading Len's first and only letter, recalling, at the same time, all the pointers there had been in the ghostly meetings with his friend which had culminated in the very last one at just after eight-thirty that morning. Eventually, he knew he had to ask his parents a vital question. He steeled himself and went downstairs. His mum had been listening for him all afternoon, not daring to enter his bedroom. She was already at the foot of the stairs to meet him. She held out her arms and said,

"How are you feeling, Eddie? Are you O.K?"

Eddie avoided his mother's clutches and said quickly,

"Do you know when Len died, Mum?"

Ann Compton could see at once that her son didn't want any motherly display of affection and, standing aside to let him pass, she replied,

"The neighbour said that it was probably just after half past eight."

Eddie smiled. The last piece of the jigsaw of ghostly clues dropped into place. His best friend's spirit had been fresh from his earthly body when Eddie had had the privilege to meet him on the beach. The fact that it had actually been after eleven that morning didn't matter. Len's ghost had arranged it to be at the same time as his death albeit nearly a year in the future. 'Clever touch, comrade', thought Eddie. 'But why hadn't he been wearing his St Christopher'?

The Comptons didn't head south until Tuesday morning. Ann finally spoke at length to Martha on Monday afternoon and, though it seemed on the surface that she was bearing up remarkably well, Ann could sense that her friend was in need of some familiar company, surrounded as she was by strangers and family she hadn't seen for years. Fred Compton still hadn't invested in a new car and the journey took the best part of six hours with only one stop for petrol in Essex. They eventually arrived at their pre-booked guest house in Petersgate at just before four in the afternoon. After a quick wash and change they were outside 23 The Park at five-thirty. Martha was clearly pleased to see them and her friend Ann in particular. Martha's sister and husband were the only family actually staying at the house. They were using the spare bedroom. The door to Len's room was closed; the room itself being still in the state it was when he had left it on the Sunday morning. Even his mother had not been in. Martha hugged her best friend on arrival.

"Thank you so much for coming. You don't know what it means to me."

There was a tear in her son's eye as Eddie replied for his mum who was crying unashamedly.

"We just had to, Aunty Martha. Len was, is and always will be my best friend as Uncle Cyril is yours."

Martha Wilby stood back from hugging her friend and, though she didn't reply to Eddie's remarkably mature eulogy, it had clearly provided her with a huge fillip as she smiled warmly at him. They both understood the other's loss.

Arrangements for the joint funerals were not to be overly delayed despite the necessary investigations that had to be concluded. The service would be held at St Michael's church on Friday, August the 27th at two-thirty. Eddie spent a lot of time until then by himself sitting in Martha's back garden. He was absolutely convinced in his own mind that he had been there before on a ghostly trip prior to the Wilby's move. Though the newly planted row of conifers was only about three feet high, they seemed to Eddie to be in exactly the same places. Even the patio area was just beyond the bottom of the lawn. Aunty Martha had been there too, of that he was certain, though she had been much older. He was equally convinced that Uncle Cyril had not. Recent events made that seem obvious. Who had been Martha's new companion?

Considering the Wilbys were so new to the area, the funeral service was very well attended on the Friday. Several of Martha's new church congregation were there despite many of them never having spoken to her – they came out of the extreme sadness that had enveloped the local community at such a tragic loss for people who had just joined their society. Though Martha didn't seem to have stayed in contact with many of her family, Cyril's side was very well represented, including both his aging parents who had travelled down by train from Scotland. The Deputy Head at Fenton Grammar School was also there accompanied by two of Eddie and Len's year group. To Martha's great surprise, 'Teddy' Crompton, Headmaster of what would have been Len's new school was also in attendance. The Banham School also sent a senior member of staff; the Head, Mr Boulter, was away on a touring holiday in France. No one came from Cyril's previous school.

Fred and Eddie had agreed to give individual eulogies for Cyril and Len and, while his son seemed strangely calm given his age and the circumstances, Fred was clearly very nervous when the vicar called him forward. Fred was brief, bland and almost clinical in his address which he read word for word from prepared notes, almost as if he was rehearsing the details of a long train journey cross country. Cyril's family didn't seem to mind; he didn't have any brothers and sisters and with the several moves needed in his profession he had few other long term friends. Martha nodded and mimed a 'thank you' when, after two minutes, Eddie's dad returned to his seat.

One of Martha's favourite hymns was followed by Eddie's eulogy. He walked confidently up to the pulpit without notes of any kind and a smile on his face which immediately lifted the sombre mood of the congregation. He looked briefly at his parents and began.

"Leonard Wilby was my best friend and he will always be so. He protected me at school when other boys tried to bully me and he gave me confidence to do those things that I often thought I couldn't do or achieve. If I had a problem, no matter how small, I could always go to Len and he would have an answer – often it wasn't the correct one but that didn't matter, even when he or I ended up in worse trouble and with a bigger headache. In Len's case, 'a problem shared was a problem doubled'."

Mild laughter relaxed the mourners. Eddie paused and continued.

"Len was not afraid to make mistakes. He was a superb sportsman, captaining both our school's football and rugby teams. He would, no doubt, have proved his prowess at his new school, Petersgate Grammar."

Mr Crompton smiled and nodded his agreement as several mourners turned to look at the well-known and respected Headmaster. Martha Wilby began to cry silently. Eddie's mum put her arm round her shoulders.

"He and I shared secrets that nobody else will ever unravel. We did things and went places that only we knew about, like all teenage boys growing up these days. Len was always the one for an adventure even when neither of us knew what the consequences would be. Len was brave and courageous and he lifted the spirits of all around him. Nobody disliked him and opposing players always respected him and shook his hand at the end of a football or rugby match. He said and did daft things at times but you couldn't wish for a better mate in a crisis. Maybe not blessed with the brain to think his way around a problem, he would often solve it with native wit and sheer strength of character. He made others

see the funny side of their predicaments. He laughed equally at himself as he did at others and...."

Eddie paused.

"*And I loved the rascal – I always will. No one could wish for a better friend and he'll be mine till I join him again in more adventures that we can now only dream about. God bless you, Len. You're a great mate, comrade.*"

Eddie's sister stood up. She put her hands together and clapped loudly. Seconds later everyone followed Jenny, not only to give thanks for Eddie's eloquence, but also as a release of pent up emotion and to express their tribute to Len when their own words couldn't possibly match the ones spoken by Eddie himself. Martha Wilby came over to Eddie and, holding his hand warmly, she whispered her own 'thank you'. She kissed his forehead lightly and returned to her seat.

The Comptons seemed to be the only non-family members to return to The Park for some sandwiches and tea after the funeral. Eddie noticed, however, that there was one man who seemed to be unattached to anyone from either side of the Wilby's families. During the wake in the garden, Martha attended to his needs more carefully than she did any of the family members – he was clearly a special friend from Martha's past. It turned out that his name was Michael Conners and he lived in London. He had been a teacher at the school that the Wilbys had once worked at in the East End; Cyril in the woodwork department and Martha as a cook. It was amazing what a fourteen-year-old boy could discover by simply standing or sitting in the most apposite position whenever Martha and Michael were talking.

Just before it was time for the Comptons to leave to return for their last night at their guest house on Petersgate's seafront, Eddie had a déjà vu experience that would provide him, and him alone, with an insight into Martha Wilby's future. Martha and Michael Conners were sitting on the patio area at the end of the garden. They were drinking tea while they discussed old times together. 'So that's who Aunty Martha's new companion had been on his earlier trip to the garden', he thought. He was glad that Martha would apparently find happiness again at some time in the future. Eddie's mother would remark later, on the drive back to Fenton-on-Sea, how happier her friend had seemed to be when talking to the tall stranger; happier than when with her own family, she would also observe.

11

The Beginning

Eddie 'saw' nothing more of his friend, Len, for the rest of the school holidays. He had gained great comfort in the knowledge that death didn't mean the end of things. Despite his love of science and the value of reasoned and logical argument, he knew he had been privileged to glimpse another world where the normal rules of such principles just didn't apply. He alone, he thought, had seen and experienced signs that told him his friendship with Len was not over. Indeed, it might only be just beginning. Surely the peeks into the future, whether real or not, had meant more than just a warning of his best friend's demise. So it was that Eddie approached the fourth year at Fenton-on-Sea Grammar School with more excitement and contentment than his family had scarcely believed would be possible. His belief that he was the only person living who had been witness to ghostly sightings was, of course, a fallacious one; his sister for one, however, had not yet realised that she had been talking to a ghost when meeting the handsome young sailor. What she had done was to keep a very careful eye on her brother in the days after his friend's death. It would be a long time before experiences would be shared between the two siblings.

The autumn term began on Monday, September the 6th and Eddie, for almost the first time ever – apart from on the rare occasion when Len had been sick – walked to school on his own. Both his teachers and fellow fourth years were instantly watchful of and sympathetic to his needs, as they were, also, to Len's many other school friends. Eddie found quickly that he was part of a fairly large clan of boys (and girls) who gained comfort in shared experiences concerning their popular schoolmate. A special assembly was held at eleven o'clock as the school's token memorial to its former pupil. It was a moving service led by Mr Smithson, the Head of Boys' P.E. and Games and while nearly every other student bowed their head's with sad expressions covering their faces, Eddie sat with a proud smile on his. In the succeeding days a memorial plaque would be put in the main corridor just before the entrance to the school gymnasium. Leonard Wilby would not be forgotten.

As usual, the term didn't really get into full swing until the following week; timetables had to be properly checked for the O-level pupils and the normal issuing and – in some cases – return of text books had to be accomplished. To his great delight, Eddie found that he had double Maths first on Monday mornings and he had his favourite teacher, Miss Ware, too. Double French and double Physics would complete what would turn out to be his favourite morning of the week. He would learn to suffer the double dose of English Language in the afternoon. It was not his favourite subject and, to make matters worse, he discovered he had 'old man' Green again, as in the previous year. His only ever detention had been provided by the irritable Head of English. Maynard Green was two years from retirement and it had begun to show; he did not suffer fools gladly and young Edward Compton fitted into such a category to a tee, he had decided. So it was that Eddie was pleasantly surprised when, at the first lesson that Monday afternoon, Mr Green seemed unusually forgiving of his incorrect and wayward answers. Eddie did not know that all his teachers had been told of his special friendship with Leonard Wilby and that they were to be careful in their dealings with him. In the previous year he and Len had always sat next to each other in English – it was the only subject for which they had been in the same set. No one had so far sat next to him in the fourth year; the adjacent seat and desk to his left had remained empty out of respect.

Towards the end of the lesson, Eddie had given a particularly errant reply to a question; so much off beam that several of his classmates giggled audibly. Mr Green looked at them sternly and said,

"Well, you lot, at least young Compton here made a stab at the answer, which is more than can be said for any of you."

"Who'd have thought old man Green would have said that, Eddie."

Eddie looked to his right to see who had spoken but it was immediately obvious that no one had – nobody would dare. The voice spoke again and it was coming from Eddie's left.

"It's me, mate."

Eddie went rigid and hardly dared look back at the empty desk beside him. He instantly knew it wouldn't be empty when eventually he did turn his head. There sat his best friend, dressed so casually that he was clearly invisible to the rest of the class. Mr Green glanced at Eddie and was about to say something before he realised that Eddie seemed to be looking wistfully at the empty seat. Maynard Green ignored Eddie's apparent inattention and carried on the debate of the prologue to Henry the Fifth.

"It's O.K., Eddie – I've just come to see how you're getting on without me this year. You don't need to say anything, mate. We mustn't get you into trouble with old 'Greeny', eh?"

Eddie kept silent. Mr Green was getting more and more anxious as Eddie continued to stare at the seat beside him.

"Meet me after school, mate. I'll see you on the way home. Go home the normal way."

Eddie nodded his head very slightly and he turned to look at his English teacher. He sensed Mr Green was staring at him.

"Are you alright, Compton?"

"Oh yes, sir. I'm absolutely fine."

He had been about to add the word 'now', but had thought better of it at the last moment. Mr Green smiled and carried on with the conclusion of the lesson. Eddie knew what he'd find when he looked back at his adjacent seat – nothing.

Eddie was understandably both nervous and excited as he walked through the school gates that afternoon. He walked up South Road as usual trying to keep to the same side of the road as he and Len had normally done. Within ten minutes he was less than fifty yards from the turning into Fir Tree Close and still his friend had not put in a ghostly appearance. Eddie began to worry that Len would leave it until he was in sight of number 38 which might cause awkward questions if anyone, especially his mum, observed him chatting to a tree! He slowed to a dawdle and started to glance over his shoulder. What would Len look like? Though in casual clothes earlier that afternoon, Eddie thought that he had looked, more or less, about the same age as when he had last seen him for real. He had reached the turn into his road. Suddenly he heard a voice call out.

"Over here, Eddie!"

Eddie looked right. There on the opposite side of South Road stood Len. He looked as though he had just come from the High Street. Eddie paused to let a cyclist pass and then crossed over the road to meet his friend. He could at last speak to him.

"Hi, Len – it's really good to see you, mate."

"You too, Captain."

Eddie wanted to hug his friend but knew it was pointless. In addition, the sight of a fourteen-year-old boy hugging thin air would have got him some very strange looks. As it was Len beckoned to Eddie to keep moving as they walked side by side towards the High Street.

"Let's find somewhere where you can talk without making people think you've gone mad," said Len soon after they'd set off together. Len seemed to want to take the lead as they walked down the High Street and headed for the beach via Steep Hill. Disconcertingly, Len clearly wanted to walk right through people thus causing Eddie to gasp in astonishment which in turn produced stares from the people that were passing. He eventually stopped his 'trick' and weaved his way onwards like a normal human being.

The tide was out when they reached the promenade and Len 'led' his friend to the water's edge not far from the spot where their first great adventure had started. Len placed himself deliberately in such a way that it would appear that Eddie was merely gazing out to sea rather than conversing with a ghost! Eddie had a question that had worried him since he had first learned of his friend's passing.

"Did it hurt, Len? I mean in the accident."

"No, mate; not a bit. I don't really remember much. Dad and I were going fishing at a place called Deal. I remember being in the car and that I thought Dad was driving too fast, but nothing else."

Eddie thought for a moment or two. He had other questions but they seemed so stupid he barely dared to ask. He asked the obvious.

"What have you been doing since you...?"

Len seemed to know the difficulty that Eddie was having in understanding what was happening and he replied,

"It's not like living on earth in the real world, mate. It's totally different. Time has no relevance; you don't measure it by days or hours but just by a series of events that happen to you. As far as I can remember I've had three so far. I remember hovering over my coffin in a strange church and hearing bits of what you said. Thanks by the way, mate. Next thing I seem to recall is sitting next to you at school in old man Green's class and setting up this meeting. Then I found myself near the station and something or someone made me arrive in South Road just as you were about to turn into Fir Tree Close. There was just nothing in between the events. I don't think I'm making them happen or making the decision to go where I go. Someone must have wanted us to meet. I'm glad they did, mate. It's really weird, you know – being a ghost."

Eddie relaxed and laughed.

"I suppose, Len, it must be a bit like when we went on our first fantastic journey when nobody could see either of us and we could move time and place quickly at speeds that were impossible for normal people."

Len also seemed to laugh.

"A bit, mate – except I don't get hungry; I don't sleep; I don't have to fulfil any other bodily functions and I can wear what I want and go where I like."

"But just now you said you haven't been in control of where you've been. Now you say you can go where you want."

"What I meant was that when I find myself in a new situation, then I can wander off where I like. I walked from the middle of the High Street to meet you, didn't I? I'm kind of just learning what I can do by myself and what is done for me. I think in time I'll be able to think myself to different places, times and events, just like...."

"Just like what, Len?"

"Just like you were able to think us to all those different places we went to on our magic carpet. Do you understand?"

"I think so. Which of the three things that have happened to you did you plan?"

"I'm not sure, Eddie. Probably I wanted to see you again and some other force engineered it for me, and you. I didn't plan to be at my own funeral – that just happened. I didn't actually plan to sit next to you at school – that just happened too, but I suspect whoever is looking after me made it possible. I was as shocked as you when I found myself next to you. We ghosts are obviously better at hiding our emotions though!"

Eddie was beginning to understand. Just then he heard a noise behind him and turned to find a dog making serious growling noises at his back. He moved a few feet to one side and immediately realised that he was not the object of the animal's displeasure. It was growling at a spot behind Eddie by the water's edge. Eddie turned back to tell his friend. There was no one to be seen. The dog stopped growling and trotted happily back up the beach to its master who shouted,

"She's alright, son. She won't bite!"

On his way back home Eddie realised that he hadn't had the chance to ask his friendly ghost some other questions concerning his other meetings with him. One bugged him all that evening. Why hadn't Len mentioned the meeting on Fenton beach that had occurred just a few minutes after his death? The other sighting of Len's ghost had been in the future, but the most recent had not, or had it? In the end, Eddie decided that, perhaps, Len hadn't mentioned anything else because, for him, the events hadn't yet happened including the one in 1966. Whatever the reason, Eddie also began to think that Len was not the only one with special powers. He himself might be able to see into the future and be aware of what Len's ghost might do before it happened.

Because of his ghostly rendezvous, Eddie eventually arrived home after five-thirty that Monday and, naturally, faced some awkward questions from his mother.

"Where have you been?" she asked as he came in through the front door.

"We had Maths club until five and I helped tidy up afterwards," he lied.

"But I thought the Maths club was on a Wednesday."

"It was last year, Mum, but that was the junior one; I'm with the fifth and sixth form now."

Eddie didn't immediately realise that he would have to invent an excuse for being home late on a Wednesday as well when the Maths club was really scheduled. He would have to face that problem later. His mother had some news for him.

"Aunty Martha phoned this afternoon; she'd been going through some of Len's things at last. There was a couple of things she thought you might like."

"Oh, Mum – like what?"

"An old railway timetable from the thirties that she said someone had given Len once for his birthday and…."

Eddie interrupted quickly.

"Did she say who had given it to him?"

"No, dear, she didn't."

Eddie breathed a sigh of relief. He would have had difficulty in explaining to his mother who Mr Jacob Manders was.

"What else did she say I might want?" said Eddie.

"Just his football that Mr Canter sent him; apparently you can still see some of the signatures on it. If you want both things she'll put them in a parcel and send them through the post."

"Tell her yes, Mum."

"O.K., Eddie."

Eddie's mum paused and then continued.

"What do you think Len was doing getting an old railway timetable? It wasn't the kind of thing he was interested in, was it? I expect your dad will want to have a look at it when it arrives."

Eddie knew immediately that he had made a mistake. His dad was bound to read the inscription inside the timetable and there was no way he could explain who Mr Manders was especially when Eddie's parents thought he was someone that the two boys had made up to get them out of a difficult situation. He thought quickly and said,

"On second thoughts, Mum, I don't think I'd like to have the timetable or football. It wouldn't feel right to have some of his things. I'd rather Aunty Martha kept them or gave them to charity."

Ann Compton looked oddly ay her son.

"Are you sure? I think Len's mum wants you to have them and she might be upset if you refuse."

'This was proving to be difficult', thought Eddie. He relented.

"Oh, O.K., Mum, I'll have them."

"That's good – I'll phone her back tomorrow."

After tea that evening, Eddie spent a good deal of time thinking about how he could prevent his dad from seeing the railway timetable. There didn't seem to be an obvious solution except one that would involve his friendly ghost. He needed to talk to Len urgently and how was he to engineer that? He had two or three days at the most and he might not see him for weeks. The opportunity would present itself the very next day.

Len was waiting in the same position on South Road when Eddie returned home from school. Eddie saw his friend immediately and quickly crossed over the road to meet him.

"Good afternoon, Captain," said Len. "I gather we have a problem."

"Yes, but how did you...?"

"How did I know? Well, we ghosts can find out lots of things without anyone knowing. I saw my mum going through my things and I was there when she phoned your mum about the timetable and football."

"Thank God," said Eddie.

"No, mate – thank *me*."

"So how can you help?"

"Already fixed, Eddie. I just haunted Mum for a few minutes so I think you'll find she's changed her mind and now she wants to keep them. I have real power, mate."

"Thanks, Len."

"No problem. I'm sorry I can't stop and talk for longer but I've things to do and places to go to. Bye!"

As before, Len immediately disappeared from sight but, this time, Eddie wasn't sure if he'd looked away from his friend for a split second or not. This was getting interesting, he thought, as he made his way home. Could he just call up his friend at will whenever he needed help? That would be good!

After school the following day, Eddie's mum told him that Martha had changed her decision to let him have the timetable and football – she was going to keep all his things as they had been in his room the day he had died. Eddie was relieved. Len was a star! With the senior Maths club being changed from a Wednesday to a Monday evening as well, Eddie began to believe that his guardian angel could also help with problems when he hadn't even asked for such assistance.

While Eddie was adjusting to his new life at school without his earthly friend, the other change in the routine of the Compton household also began the following day, the 16th of September. Jenny started her beauty therapy course at Hamsden Civic College. Sam Arleson still wanted her to work at his baker's shop on Saturdays and in the holidays. Equipment for her course had already cost her and, indeed, her parents, well over a hundred pounds. She was a bit nervous when she boarded the bus – the cheaper of the two forms of transport – on the Thursday morning. This apprehension was not only because it was her first day at college but also because it was the first time she had travelled to Hamsden by bus since her meeting with the young sailor. Apart from her brother, she had still not mentioned that meeting to anyone.

12

A Ghostly Day Out

Though Eddie tried hard over the next few weeks to urge his friend to put in another appearance, he had no success. By the middle of October he was beginning to think that he would never reappear, even when he might desperately need him for some crisis or other. However, when Friday, October the 15th dawned unusually warm and sunny, Eddie's hopes of another liaison were strangely lifted. Whether it was the summery weather, reminding him of the last such meeting, or the fact that, like Monday, his school day would conclude with English, he wouldn't be able to decide. He just knew something would happen that day. He couldn't wait for his English lesson with Mr Green to start. But he knew there could be a problem. Sally Barber had taken to sitting next to him in Len's old place – she had only started at Fenton Grammar that term and thus had no qualms about sitting in the seat next to Eddie. Eddie had a plan to prevent her doing so, but he knew he had to get to room 46 before anyone else, including Mr Green, if he was to carry it out.

As usual, everyone in Mr Green's fourth year English class was silent on entry to room 46, until Sally Barber's voice echoed round the room.

"Sir? Sir?"

"Yes, Miss Barber and what is the problem?"

"Sir, someone's spilt ink all over my seat and desk."

"Well go and sit somewhere else."

"Yes, sir."

Mr Green came over to the back row to inspect the desk and chair. He stood right beside Eddie.

"Are you responsible for this, Compton?"

"No, sir. I don't use black ink as you know, sir. It was like it when I got here. It probably happened over lunchtime."

Eddie sat nervously hoping that Mr Green wouldn't ask to look in his bag where lurked an empty bottle of black fountain pen ink specially bought at lunchtime for the purpose. Maynard Green just grunted. It was Friday afternoon and he couldn't be bothered to investigate further. He would inform the caretaker later. He walked back to his normal position at the front of the room.

"*So, set four, we return to Act Four, Scene Two.*"

Eddie didn't really hear anything that was said over the next ten minutes or so. His mind was elsewhere as his eyes glanced constantly to his left. He was fortunate that Mr Green didn't ask him any questions and that he didn't notice his fidgety behaviour. Copious amounts of blotting paper lay in place soaking up most of the black liquid. Would Len get it on his clothes? As Eddie was posing the question in his mind, he looked briefly to the front. When he turned back, there was Len sitting in the ink-covered chair. He was smiling broadly.

"*Good trick, mate,*" he said loudly – indeed, so loudly that Eddie thought everyone would hear. The class carried on as normal. Eddie was about to whisper something when Len continued.

"*Don't say a word. Just listen.*"

Eddie gave the barest of nods.

"*Fancy a day out tomorrow, Eddie. Put your left hand on the desk for yes.*"

Eddie's left hand appeared on his desk.

"*Are you doing anything special?*"

Eddie replaced his left hand with his right. The code worked!

"*Meet me outside the station at nine. I have plans.*"

Left hand changed to right. Mr Green had spotted Eddie's inattention.

"Concentrate please, Mr Compton. You have homework on this scene over the weekend."

"Yes, sir – sorry, sir."

"Is that ink bothering you? You seem to be more interested in that than Shakespeare."

"It's just a bit smelly, sir."

"Well, please pay attention, Compo. I won't tell you again."

"Yes, sir."

Eddie looked down at his copy of Henry the Fifth. Out of the corner of his left eye he could see that the chair next to him was empty.

Saturday was as pleasantly warm as the previous day; an Indian summer had arrived in Fenton-on-Sea. Eddie prepared his parents by informing them he would likely be out for most of the day. As Fred Compton was leaving for work at the station, he inquired,

"Where are you off to today, then, son?"

"Thought I might go to Hamsden for the day. Town are at home this afternoon."

"You may have to come back on the bus. Engineering work starts on the track near Linham Junction this evening. What train are you going to catch this morning?"

"The ten past nine, I expect. Depends on…."

"Depends on what?" said Eddie's mum.

Eddie thought quickly. He'd nearly said the wrong thing.

"Depends on whether I want to go that early, Mum."

It seemed a lame qualification to his statement and his mother looked a little oddly at him, but instead she asked,

"What about your lunch? Do you want me to make you some sandwiches?"

"No, I'll get something in Hamsden."

Eddie's mother seemed satisfied but, nevertheless, she still smiled knowingly. She thought she knew what Eddie had been originally planning to say. Her son must have his first girlfriend.

"Well have a good day. You'll have to get a move on – it's quarter to already."

Eddie managed to get to the station forecourt just as St Andrew's church clock sounded the hour. Len didn't seem to be in sight. The clock finished striking and Eddie wandered towards the station entrance. A strange sight suddenly greeted him. His dad was walking side by side with his best friend. Fred Compton spotted his son and came up to him accompanied by Len at his side. Eddie's friend grinned cheekily but it was Eddie's dad who spoke.

"Just off for my paper while there's a lull – I'm showing young Dave the ropes this morning."

"Come on, mate, I want to catch the ten past train."

Eddie wasn't sure who to reply to first, but managed,

"Have to go, Dad; it's five past."

"See you later, son."

"See you later, Mr Compton."

Eddie turned and waited until his dad was out of earshot.

"That was not nice," he said to Len.

"Sorry, mate – it was just a bit of fun. I'd been to check the train times and saw your dad on the way out."

Eddie bought a day return to Hamsden from Dave Barton and just managed to catch the ten past nine train from platform one. Hamsden was where Eddie's ghostly friend wanted to go as well. The train was packed with Saturday morning shoppers and Eddie couldn't find two seats until Len whispered,

"I don't need a seat, mate!"

Eddie found one vacant seat in the front carriage next to a young blond girl of about his own age. Len promptly sat on her lap! Eddie looked totally shocked. Len leant over and whispered in his ear.

"Bet you wish you could do this, eh?"

The blond girl couldn't see or feel anything. Eddie sat in silence and waited. He didn't have to wait long for Len's 'plan' to begin. The ten pat nine train was one of the few trains that stopped at Linmouth Junction and as it began to slow down, Len got up and headed for the door. Eddie followed. No one noticed that the door appeared to open of its own accord a split second before Eddie turned the handle. Eddie jumped off the train and followed his friend to the end of the single platform.

"What are you doing, Len?"

"Want to go for a walk, mate. I want to see if we can see Ally Grant or that other bloke we met – the one in the white coat. Something about him bothered me."

There was no point not telling his friend now, thought Eddie but he started cautiously.

"You mean you don't know who he was?"

"No. Should I?"

"I saw the lapel badge he was wearing."

"So what did it say?"

"It read *Dr Leonard Wilby*. I mean, Doctor! You would never have become a doctor, mate."

Len's ghost didn't reply. Eddie offered an explanation.

"You know what I think, Len?"

Len shook his head. He was clearly disturbed.

"I think we met your ghost many years in the future and it was in a guise of someone that you always wanted to be – a nuclear scientist."

"I never wanted to be a scientist. I only ever wanted to be a professional sportsman and, anyway, you might have wanted to see my name on the lapel badge. It might have just been mind association. I was with you at the time, remember?"

"Yes, but maybe ghosts age and you somehow 'became' the scientist or you can change into someone else just by thinking about it."

"Maybe. I haven't tried it yet."

"Are you sure, Len?"

"I think so. Why?"

"Because I met you on Fenton beach on the day you died except it wasn't 1965 it was 1966, I think."

Eddie still could not remember what Len's ghost had talked about and it was also soon obvious to him that Len had no recollection of the event either.

"No way, Eddie. The first time I saw you in the flesh was at my funeral."

Eddie shrugged his shoulders.

"As I said, it was in the future, like when I saw the old scientist and, anyway, even though you seem to be in control of your actions as a ghost, you are still a ghost."

"What do you mean?"

"I just mean that how we see ghosts is probably different from how you want to be seen. The sightings that you don't remember were meant for me alone and they may never actually happen to you. And…."

"And?"

"And there maybe more than one of you; at least three I should say!"

Eddie's sister would have shouted, 'Four!' very loudly if she had been able. Len smiled.

"That would be good, but surely I'd know what my other ghosts were doing."

"Not necessarily, mate. Your separate apparitions could live in their own worlds, independent of each other."

"Pretty good this dying lark, eh? I can be as many people as I like now. I could even play football for Tottenham one day."

"You're not in control, Len. It's not your choice, I hope. God is in charge."

Eddie debated inwardly whether to tell his friend about the young fair-haired Tottenham reserve footballer, called L Wilton, or about his sister's possible sighting, but decided against it on both counts.

Without realising it, Eddie and his ghostly friend had been walking for a few minutes and had reached the level crossing through which they had seen the other world of the nuclear power station. Even Len didn't seem confident about crossing the railway line.

"I'd better go first, Eddie. Any real person won't be able to see me, but there might be a problem if there's another one of my species over the other side. Wait for about a minute before you come."

Eddie waited until Len had reached the other side of the railway line and he was relieved when he didn't seem to have disappeared from view. Eddie timed a minute on his watch and then ventured across too. Immediately he reached the other side the weather and time of day changed completely. It was twilight and icy cold; the ground was frost-covered. Eddie's watch still read five past ten. Len was nowhere to be seen. A man in a white coat was approaching and Eddie feared who it would be. Dr Leonard Wilby looked the same as he had the last time Eddie had seen him. He said more or less the same thing too.

"I'm sorry but you can't come any further. This area is restricted."

This time Eddie did not turn and run.

"Hello, Len."

"Do I know you, young man?"

"It's Eddie – Eddie Compton. We both lived in Fenton-on-Sea when we were boys."

Dr Wilby frowned.

"Eddie Compton, you say? Why yes, I do remember you before we moved to Kent and I...."

Eddie was excited. This was a new twist.

"Really? What do you remember?"

"Well, let me see. I remember you were clever at school and I also seem to remember something very strange happened to us, but I just can't...."

Dr Wilby again didn't finish. Suddenly he shook violently and looked to be about to shout or scream something but a flash of bright light hid his body from Eddie for a fleeting moment. Almost at once the normal twilight returned. Dr Wilby had gone and Len was standing in front of Eddie.

"Hi, Eddie. Where've you been?"

"I followed you straightaway but you'd disappeared."

"I only went about a hundred yards up the road. When I turned round, you seemed to be talking to thin air, so I came back to see what you were doing. Who *were* you talking to?"

"You!"

"Me?"

"Yes – Dr Leonard Wilby. It was like before at the nuclear power station and it was winter."

Eddie looked round as he was speaking. It was a beautiful autumn morning.

"I think you're beginning to see ghosts, Eddie!" said Len's ghost.

"I have three words for you, comrade Len."

"What?"

"Pot, kettle and black."

Len grinned widely.

"You mean the old scientist was me?"

"Yes, I suppose he must have been another of your ghosts, but in forty or fifty years time. Both times I've seen him, he spoke with your voice, only older."

"Why don't I know anything about it?"

"Because it hasn't happened yet. I was just given a glimpse into the future, like we looked into the past when we saw old Granty and it was about 1910. Obviously at some point in the future you will decide that you fancy being a nuclear scientist."

Len seemed to be satisfied with Eddie's explanation.

"I'd rather be a footballer!"

Eddie smiled.

"Anyway," Len continued. "I came here to see if we could find Mr Aloyisious Grant."

"Why, in particular?"

"He's the only other ghost that I might be able to talk to in this locality. He didn't die much before I did; it would only be about eighteen months ago. The only other ghost is Mr Manders and he must have been dead for a hundred years."

"Have you not seen your dad yet, then?" asked Eddie.

"No. I don't want him to be a ghost. I don't fancy him haunting me."

Eddie didn't know whether to laugh or cry. He thought he might have touched a nerve with Len. He tried to look on the funny side.

"How can one ghost haunt another ghost? I thought you were all supposed to belong to the same union."

Len's reaction told Eddie immediately that ghosts didn't have the same emotions as their human counterparts.

"I'm just a beginner at this game, mate, so I don't have the same feelings as you. I don't feel sad that my dad's dead and he doesn't haunt me. I only have good memories of him."

After their discussion on the behaviour and characteristics of ghosts, Eddie and Len decided to recross the railway line; there was no sign of anyone else in sight on their side of the crossing – whether human or not. As they walked back to the platform at Linham Junction, Len had some bad news.

"We have a problem that I forgot to mention to you, Eddie."

"Oh yeah?"

"Yes – when I checked the times of the trains that actually stop here on a Saturday, I found that there isn't another one until three-thirty this afternoon and that still goes to Hamsden."

"So have we got to wait until then to get to Hamsden?" asked Eddie.

"We? I don't have to wait to get anywhere, mate!"

Eddie thought for a moment.

"Do you reckon you could get us both to Hamsden, Len?"

"How?"

"What about you trying to think us there?"

127

Len stopped walking. They had reached the isolated station at Linham Junction.

"I suppose so, but I'm not sure what I can do though."

"Just think of Hamsden."

"Unfortunately, Eddie, I don't think like real people. I can't plan things in my mind. I can only concentrate on things that are right in front of me. Everything else is a bit of a haze."

"Do you remember Hamsden?"

"Vaguely. What did we do there?"

"Went shopping when we couldn't get what we wanted in Fenton."

Len screwed up his ghostly face trying to remember. Eddie thought of something.

"Your dad bought his new car from Richard Jones' Cars in Hamsden."

Though Len hadn't been with his parents when they had purchased the doomed vehicle, it did seem to jog something in Len's ghostly brain.

"I remember a big shop, Eddie. I think it was called Osborne's. I bought some toys from there once when I was small. Is there a shop called that in Hamsden?"

Eddie smiled and said,

"Yes. It's the biggest department store there. All you've got to do is th…."

But Len had already been thinking of it and suddenly they were pitched into darkness. Eddie would remember later that he'd had the distinct feeling that someone or something had touched his arm. A second later and light returned, albeit of a subtly different kind. It was man-made. Eddie looked round; he was inside a department store.

Once his eyes had adjusted to the shop lighting, Eddie focused properly on his new surroundings. Len didn't seem to be with him. Had he made the trip? He walked a few paces towards a shop counter; it was the toy department. Suddenly he heard a familiar voice.

"Hello, Eddie. It is you, isn't it?"

Eddie didn't at first look in the direction of the voice; it wasn't the kind of thing that Len would have said given they had only just been together a minute or two earlier.

"Thought it was. How are you, mate?"

Eddie turned and looked to his left. It was Len, but this version seemed to be two or three years older.

"Len?"

"Yes – who did you think it was?"

"I don't know. It's just that you look much older than when I last saw you."

"I'm seventeen now."

Eddie relaxed when he heard the word 'now'. It was another of his friend's ghostly guises come back to haunt him.

"Where did you just come from?" asked Eddie cautiously.

"I don't know. My mind's a blank, mate."

Another voice entered the conversation.

"Who *are* you talking to, Eddie?"

Eddie turned to his right. It was the familiar version of his best friend. There stood Len's younger ghost dressed as he had been when they had been at Linham Junction. Len's older ghost then said,

"What did you say, Eddie?"

Eddie didn't turn back and answered the first question.

"You're not going to believe this but I've just been talking to another version of you, but he's older. Look behind me, Len."

Len peered past his friend's shoulder and said,

"There's no one there, Captain – at least no one that could be me. Not a nice one anyway."

Eddie turned round. The older Len was still standing in the same position. He was waiting for an answer to *his* question and then it dawned on Eddie. Neither ghost could see the other! Eddie turned back to the younger Len.

"Just a moment, Len."

Eddie turned away from his friend.

"Go away, please, I'm busy."

"Oh, don't be like that, Eddie; I'm your friend."

"No you're not, you're a bad ghost."

"You think so, eh? I'll show you how bad I can be; just wait and see."

The 'evil' ghost vanished instantly. Eddie knew he had guessed right. You couldn't have two 'good' ghosts – evil always opposed good.

"What was that all about, mate?" queried Len.

"Although you couldn't see him, there was another ghost, but I knew he wasn't you. He just looked how you might have looked if you were about seventeen."

By now, quite a few people had witnessed Eddie's odd behaviour as he constantly turned left and right and talked to empty air. The young lady assistant behind the counter said,

"Are you alright?"

"Oh yes, just talking to myself. Sorry! Couldn't make up my mind which way to go."

Eddie didn't know it but he had been fortunate that the shop assistant had been too far away to hear exactly what he'd said. She, of course, had not seen nor heard anyone else.

The 'real' Len had already moved some distance away from Eddie and he beckoned to him to join him. Once Eddie was out of earshot of anyone else who might have heard his weird and one-sided conversation, Len said,

"I think that bloke over there heard some of what you said and he's talking to one of the shop security staff."

"It wouldn't have made much sense to him," said Eddie.

"Exactly! All the more reason for him to get you certified insane! Let's get out of here."

Once they were outside and hidden in the anonymity of the Saturday shoppers, Eddie spoke in some detail about his conversation with Len's 'bad' ghost. Len had a theory to explain its existence.

"We're all made up of a good side and a bad side, mate. I'm the ghost of my good side, but somewhere out there there's a ghost who represents my bad side. Stick we me, Captain."

"Don't worry, comrade; I will. I sent the other one packing."

Len looked tired as though the morning's events had taken a lot out of him.

"Good show, Eddie. I'll have to go now; I'm tired, but I'll see you again soon."

Before Eddie had a chance to say anything, Len became a blur in the crowd of shoppers. He had gone. Eddie looked at his watch and he couldn't really believe his eyes. It was ten past two.

Eddie still saw the game at Freeman Street after he had grabbed a bite to eat consisting of a pie and chips ate at a café next to the ground. Town lost 2–1, but Eddie's spirits were not dampened after his earlier excitement. However, in the train on the way home, a couple of thoughts came to him which were not altogether pleasant. Firstly, what *could* the 'evil' ghost do to him when he'd promised to show him how bad he could be? Though this was frightening and disconcerting enough, the second thought hardly bore thinking about. What if Len's younger ghost was actually the bad ghost and the seventeen-year-old version was the good one?

13

Return to Petersgate

Over the next few days, Eddie began to realise the enormity of what Len had been able to do with his instant space travel, even though it had only been about six miles. Of course, such a thing was not new to Eddie, or Len, but when it had happened before both of them had been alive. Now, Len didn't exist and he himself, who did, had accompanied him!

The autumn half-term arrived on Friday, October the 29th and Eddie had been looking forward to it with some anticipation. Would his friend pay him another visit? What had he been doing in the time since the Hamsden trip? Nothing had happened at school – no ghostly classmates sitting beside him or meeting him on the way home. By the Saturday morning, Eddie began to put his own plans into operation, starting with some homework up until lunch, because of the weather and because his sister was out with her boyfriend, Gary, so the house would not be blaring with loud music. That would be followed, in the afternoon, by a trip to Hamsden with his dad to buy a new car. Fred Compton's green Morris Minor 1000 had finally all but given up the ghost. It had hardly been used since late August when Eddie's dad had first made the decision to get rid of the rust bucket. Fred Compton didn't like spending money, especially large amounts, and his slowness in making the decision mirrored this reluctance.

So it was that, at a little after two, Eddie and his dad climbed into VAP 205 and headed for Richard Jones' showroom in Hamsden.

"What are we going to get, Dad," asked Eddie as they crawled onto the A132 at all of thirty-five miles an hour.

"Don't know, son. Let's see what he's got first. I'm not buying today."

Eddie knew he had to persuade his dad to change that decision before they reached Hamsden – he was sure that his mum had been keen for him to accompany his dad for the very reason that she knew that her husband would be reluctant to come to a decision. Eddie had to push his dad into a deal that day and no later.

"We'll be lucky to get this old girl to the showroom, Dad."

"It'll get there – it's never let me down yet."

Eddie stared to put the pressure on. Emotional blackmail could be the key.

"We don't want to have an accident though, like…."

Eddie's dad didn't reply at first. He knew what his son had been about to say. Eventually he said,

"That happened because they were going too fast. This thing struggles to get to fifty now."

"Precisely, Dad. Sometimes you need a bit of speed to get out of situations that have been caused by someone else's bad driving."

"Maybe, Eddie. You seem to know a lot about driving a car given you don't drive one."

Eddie thought he had done enough. He didn't want to antagonise his dad further. He said nothing more until his dad pulled the car onto the forecourt of Richard Jones' Cars. He made up a little white lie.

"He had some nice cars in the other Saturday when I came with…."

Eddie suddenly felt himself sweating.

"Who did you come with last time, Eddie?"

"Oh, I just met Tom Dunn on the way to the match and we stopped to look in the window."

Eddie's dad seemed satisfied and they got out of the old Morris. Eddie breathed an inward sigh of relief. Mr Richard Jones seemed surprised to see Fred and his son.

"Good morning, Fred. Jenny's gone out with Gary for the day, I'm afraid, if you were looking for her. She didn't say you'd be coming."

"No, Richard – She'd probably forgotten. We've come to look for a car."

"Well, it's the end of the month so you've come at the right time if you want a good deal. It's about time you got rid of that old banger of yours. It'll soon be a vintage motor. What are you looking for?"

"Oh, I don't know. What have you got? I don't want anything similar to what you sold Cyril Wilby."

"No, I quite understand, but the tragic accident was nothing to do with the car. It was mechanically sound and tested. I had the Kent police round, you know. They told me that the brakes had worked as well as they could, given the speed the car had been doing. They can tell that from the skid marks."

"Yes, I know, Richard. You cannot possibly hold yourself to blame in any way, but I would prefer something not quite as fast or sporty."

"O.K., Fred. Let me see what I can show you."

Richard Jones walked over to the back of the showroom.

"Here we are – this might suit you. It's a two-tone Hillman Minx; 1600 hundred engine; top speed about seventy-eight and it's only just a year old with less than 10,000 on the clock. Nice ember-red and cream."

Since Eddie had been walking directly behind his dad and Mr Jones, he saw the car last, but it wasn't the car that caught his eye first. Sitting on the bonnet was Len's good ghost. He smiled when he saw Eddie and put a finger to his lips. Eddie wandered to look at another car while Len followed. Out of earshot Len said quickly,

"I'll see you tonight in your bedroom, about nine."

Immediately he had finished this instruction, he disappeared and Eddie strolled nonchalantly back to the two men.

"Seen something else, young Eddie?" asked Mr Jones.

"No, I think the Hillman looks nice."

An hour later and Comptons senior and minor were on their way back to Fenton-on-Sea; all the paperwork had been completed and Eddie's dad would take delivery of his new Hillman in about a week. He had spent more than he had wanted to but not more than he had budgeted for at worst. His son seemed preoccupied on the return journey.

"You're quiet, Eddie. Didn't you like the car?"

"Sorry, Dad. What did you say?"

"I said: did you not like the car?"

"Oh yes, Dad. I was just thinking of something else."

Eddie's dad did not pursue his questioning. He had learned over the previous weeks not to disturb his son's 'quiet moments' since the loss of his best friend.

It was eight-thirty and Eddie had made the excuse that he wanted to do some reading in his bedroom. Both his parents fully understood his need to have his own space and not only because he still missed Len, but also because it was a natural phase of growing up. In future, he would very rarely spend Saturday evenings watching television with his mum and dad.

At ten to the hour, he locked his door and sat on his bed. Which Len would appear? He needn't have worried as Len's younger version arrived dead (?) on cue at nine o'clock. Eddie had been standing looking out of his window at the night sky and, when he turned back, there was his friend sitting on his bed, grinning like a Cheshire cat.

"Very punctual, comrade," said Eddie.

"I don't have a watch, mate. It would appear that my good half can dictate precisely when I should become visible. I've told you before that nothing happens to me between such visitations. I just move from one to the next. It's an easy life."

"So what do you want, Len?"

"I've come to ask a favour of you."

"How on earth can I help you?"

"I want you to come on another trip with me – only a slightly longer one this time."

"Where?"

"Petersgate. I want to go and see my mum."

Eddie looked a little puzzled.

"I thought you said you didn't have feelings."

"I don't, at least not in the same way as you, but I just want to see how she's getting on. She lost her husband and her only son after all."

"Why do you need me to come, Len?"

"There are two reasons. Firstly, you're my best friend and secondly, I'd like you to see my new house and garden."

Eddie nearly said, 'I've seen the garden', but instead replied,

"Alright, I'll come. When did you have in mind?"

"How about next Saturday, whatever date that will be?"

"It'll be the 6th of November."

"November? And here's me thinking it was still summer."

"You mean you don't know what month it is?"

"No, as I said, I move from event to event. Time has no relevance. It just stands still and I can't get older unless my good side needs me to for some purpose or other. Right now I'm the still the same age as you, but maybe I'll be older in the future."

"I've already seen a couple of older versions of you, one of which still worries me."

"Which one?"

"The seventeen-year-old evil version I met in Osborne's."

"Don't worry about him; I can deal with him. I'll show him how bad I can be too."

Something jogged Eddie's memory but before he had time to remember, Len said,

"Got to go; I'm tired. See you next Saturday. Be ready at nine outside the station."

Len's image vanished in a blur. Eddie sat down on the bed. It felt cold. He was trembling. Eddie cast his mind back to the Saturday that he and 'Len' had been at Osborne's in Hamsden. The other ghost had said more or less the same thing as his friend had just said: '*I'll show you how bad I can be*'. Worse than that, thought Eddie, the good Len had added the word 'too', which meant that Len's good ghost had at least heard the bad one and probably must have seen him too, despite his denial. The good Len had lied which meant that he might not be....

Eddie was understandably cautious when he met Len on the following Saturday and, during the week before, he'd already made the decision that he would not go anywhere with Len until he had asked him about his apparent lie. Len seemed to know that something was on Eddie's mind.

"Good morning, Eddie. You look a bit worried."

They stood together on the station forecourt and Eddie said,

"I don't think you were quite truthful about not seeing your evil ghost in Osborne's."

Len smiled guiltily.

"I know I wasn't mate."

"Why not?"

"Because, at the time, I didn't know what *you'd* seen and heard. I didn't want you being scared so I hoped you would just think it was a trick or something."

Eddie wasn't convinced.

"But why didn't you say something afterwards, instead of pretending you hadn't seen him?"

"I did, Eddie. I tried to explain who the other ghost might have been. Remember, I'm as new to this game as you are. It was as much of a shock to me to see an older me standing behind you! I'm sorry I didn't say I'd seen him; I was scared too, you know. I just wanted to get away and think, like, I expect, you did this week."

Eddie began to relax; his friendly ghost's explanation seemed to be plausible. It was a difficult thing to know if a ghost was lying when they didn't exist in the first place!

Len had already turned away but not towards the station as Eddie imagined he would do. Instead, he seemed to float out of the forecourt and back up the High Street. Eddie followed but had difficulty in keeping up. Where was his friend going? He just about managed to keep him in sight until, at last, he realised where the ghost was bound. Eddie slowed to a walk and caught up with Len outside his old house in Lime Tree Avenue.

"What have you come here for?" asked Eddie as he reached his friend who was leaning against number 7. "You didn't live here when you died, you know."

Eddie thought for a moment that his friend had had a memory lapse, but Len soon corrected him.

"I know, stupid, but I thought I'd like to see my old house first. It's been painted, you know."

"I didn't – I haven't been up here since you left. What are we going to do now? It's getting a bit awkward for me just loitering outside your old house."

"I need to try and focus on my mum and being here helps. Strangely enough, I can't really remember what she looks like. I just have a sense of her – a warm feeling inside."

Len looked wistfully up to the window of what had been his parents' bedroom and suddenly Eddie was blinded by a flash of bright white light. A second later and normal daylight returned. He found himself standing in the familiar garden in Petersgate. It took a few seconds for his eyes to adjust back to the light which was provided by the weak autumn sunshine. The garden looked a little unkempt since the last time he had seen it after the funerals. Eddie began walking towards the house where he presumed Len had gone after he had arrived. He got to within ten yards of the lounge window when he spotted the back door begin to open. Not knowing who it would be, he dived for cover behind a holly bush to his left. It was Martha Wilby and she was heading for what looked like a small shed at the side of the garden behind him. He knew that he would never be able to explain his sudden appearance in her garden so as she passed him, he dived the other way and made for the open door. He prayed that he could find the front door and that it would open quickly and easily. Fortunately the back door led into the kitchen whose other door opened onto the hall. A couple of seconds later and he flung himself at the front door and into the small front garden beyond. There was still no sign of Len and he was getting nervous. He completed his escape by walking nonchalantly down the front path and out into the road. Nobody seemed to be about in The Park. He crossed over the road and waited outside number 24 where, to his relief, he could stand beside a telephone box without drawing attention to himself. Where was Len? Had he gone into the house? Another possibility was forming in Eddie's mind. Had Len reached Petersgate at all?

After five minutes, a female resident from number 26 came to use the phone. Eddie strolled away until he was about fifty yards from the box but still able to see number 23. At first, he didn't see Len emerge from Martha's house. He just seemed to appear in the front garden as though he'd been spirited there from somewhere else. Eddie tried to attract his attention without causing a disturbance of any kind. Len saw him and started to walk across the road. He looked happy. He got half-way and a passing cyclist rode straight through him. Len didn't deviate from his original course and reached Eddie completely unscathed.

"A man on a cycle rode right through you, Len," said Eddie once they had been reunited.

"Didn't feel a thing, mate."

"Where've you been?" asked a relieved Eddie.

"Well, when I arrived here I found myself in mum's lounge and she was sitting on the sofa. She must have sensed something. I think she may have felt I was there, you know, Eddie. She kept looking nervously round the room and eventually she went out the back door and into the garden. When she came back she was carrying an old piece of wood and she proceeded to search the room as though she was looking for a …."

"Looking for what?"

"A mouse or something, I suppose. A couple of times she seemed to pass right through me and, Eddie, I could smell her perfume. I'm sure of it."

"I expect she mistook your presence for the type of noise a small animal would make. You could be right, mate," agreed Eddie. "What did you do then?"

"After she had decided that there was no mouse, she sat back on the sofa and carried on with her knitting. It was just like old times, Eddie, and she looked happy and content. The house looks tidy and well-cared for. She's going to be alright, Eddie. I'm so pleased."

"Did you go anywhere else in the house?"

"I went into my bedroom and she's changed it. It's just a spare room now and she's got her sewing machine in there too."

"Doesn't that make you sad, Len?"

"No it doesn't. It means Mum is beginning to get over her losses and is starting a new life. That makes me happy."

Eddie looked sad and uneasy.

"Come on, cheer up, Eddie. Death's not the end of the world! Let me show you a bit of Petersgate before I spirit us back to Fenton-on-Sea. How long have you got today?"

"I'd like to be back by lunchtime; Dad's collecting his new car this afternoon and I'm supposed to be going with him and Mum."

"No problem. What's the time now?"

Eddie looked at his watch.

"Five past ten."

"Excellent – we should have plenty of time to see the sights."

As usual, Len took the lead out of The Park and he headed initially for the beach via a series of side streets that ran off the Canterbury road. He seemed to float over the ground and Eddie again had some difficulty in keeping up. Petersgate didn't have a promenade as such, Eddie discovered; the road was bordered by a low sea wall with a pebbly beach on the other side. Eddie soon noticed something else too – the smell.

"What's that horrible smell?" he asked as he peered over the sea wall. Len replied,

"The seaweed. Dad said it would be good as a fertiliser for the garden. They clear it in the summer months, but it's left to just rot this time of the year, unless a storm or high tide washes it away."

Eddie looked out to sea and then said,

"Fenton-on-Sea is over there; nothing but sea between here and there."

Half an hour later and Len had led Eddie to Petersgate Grammar School in Front Street. Eddie was obviously impressed with the old buildings.

"Looks posh, Len."

"Maybe from the outside; it was alright inside. At least the Head, Mr Crompton seemed to be nicer than old 'Hempers'.

Eddie looked at the Head's name on the board outside the main gate; so similar to his own. Was it just a coincidence? Len broke his thoughts.

"Well there we are, I never actually got to go here, mate, but Mr Crompton came to my funeral. That was good of him, wasn't it?"

"Yes, it was," said Eddie. "We ought to be getting on if you're going to show me anything else."

"Just the town and the cemetery at St Michael's where Dad and I are buried. I can show you my grave. Won't that be spooky?"

"No," said Eddie with a grimace.

They walked quickly down into the town which, though more compact than Fenton, seemed to Eddie to have more and a greater variety of shops. Just for fun, Eddie bought a souvenir postcard of Petersgate to take home with him. Len wasn't happy with his friend's purchase.

"You shouldn't do that, you know."

"Why not?"

"Because you don't seem to realise that today's trip with me can't be real in your earthly sense. You were spirited here with a ghost, mate!"

"I just want to see if the postcard stays with me when I get home or whether it disappears."

"It'll vanish. Don't you worry about that."

"We'll see," said Eddie with a smile.

The visit to St Michaels' church cemetery seemed to be more poignant and sad to Eddie than to his friendly ghost, who, on arrival, said nonchalantly,

"That's where I am, Captain. Dad's next to me."

Simple named and dated gravestones had been erected above the grassed mounds. Eddie felt a cold shiver go up his back as he glanced at his friend. Len seemed to be struggling to stay upright. Suddenly, he toppled forward and became a blur that hovered horizontally above the grave and then vanished completely. Eddie shouted involuntarily,

"Come back! Len, come back!"

Eddie looked round anxiously. The small church cemetery was empty of anybody else, human or otherwise. He wandered frantically round and round Len's grave murmuring,

"Oh God, he's gone back into his coffin. Oh God!"

He stopped his manic movement. He tried to calm down and think about the situation logically. Immediately he remembered his own words that he'd spoken to his friend on a previous occasion when they had been discussing the philosophical side of the behaviour of ghosts. In his mind he repeated some of what he'd said.

'*You're not in control, Len ... God is in charge*'.

Eddie felt both reassured and totally distraught. How was he to get back home? What could he say about where he'd been? God had taken Len back to his grave and he alone knew when he would release him again. They had tampered with things beyond their comprehension and this was the result – his worst nightmare. What could he do? Then a thought came to him. He had to pray to God, even though he'd never really believed in him, apart from the times, often before Christmas, when he'd wished in his mind for the present he really wanted. Was that prayer? He could remember vaguely the Reverend Weaver saying something about having faith and belief in God if you prayed. You had to truly believe that God, and only God, could answer your prayers. Eddie fell to his knees. He had always really known that it had been God that had shown him and Len all the fantastic things they had seen. He *did* believe even though he would find it difficult to admit it to anyone else, but he did, there and then, admit it to himself.

"Oh God, I do believe that you can bring Len back and help me to get home. Please help me. I know you're the only one I can turn to. I put my trust in you. Amen."

"What *are* you doing, mate?"

Len's voice echoed in Eddie's head. He opened his eyes and looked to his right. There, towering over him, was Len.

"Oh, thank God! I thought you'd gone back into your grave."

Len looked bemused.

"I don't know what happened. It just went black for a moment as if I was moving to my next appearance like before. Then I found myself standing on Fenton beach and you were kneeling beside me."

Having had his eyes closed while he had made his supplication, Eddie hadn't really been conscious of his environment. He put his hand down by his knees and felt wet sand. He stood up and looked all around him. Len was right. It was Fenton-on-Sea beach and they were right by the pier. He looked at his watch. It was twelve-thirty. 'Thank God', he thought. 'Len had come back'.

"Oh that was really scary, Len," he said.

Len did not reply. He was nowhere in sight.

14

A Shared Secret

Eddie just managed to get home by one o'clock and after a quick lunch he joined his mum and dad for the ride to Hamsden to change their car. Once again his dad commented on his quietness.

"Are you alright, son? What did you get up to this morning?"

"Not much, just a long walk on the promenade and a bit of shopping in Hamsden."

"What did you buy?" asked his mum.

"Nothing much, but I did find an old postcard shop and they had one of Petersgate which I bought for two shillings – a bit expensive but it'll remind me of Len."

"Have you got it with you?"

"Yes, it's in my pocket."

Eddie knew he was pushing his luck as he hadn't bothered to see whether the postcard he'd bought in Kent was still there, but he could always say he'd lost it or left it at home. He reached in his back pocket and handed the card to his mum.

"And this cost you two shillings? It's got three pence written in pencil on the back."

"The man in the shop said it was more because it wasn't a local scene."

"Why didn't you let me ask Aunty Martha? She would have got you eight for the price you paid for this. Such a waste, Eddie."

"Yes, Mum; I just bought it on the spur of the moment, I suppose."

Eddie was even quieter on the rest of the journey to Hamsden. This was incredible – something tangible from his paranormal visit to Kent. It was scientifically impossible, but the proof was in his hands. He studied the back more closely as his dad drove onto the showroom forecourt. He was relieved that his mum had not also seen the shop's name printed in tiny lettering in the top left hand corner:

M.K.Johnson Stationers

25 Lower Front Street

Petersgate

Kent

"Come on, Eddie, you can't stay in the car. You'll end up at the scrapyard."

Mr Richard Johnson was holding the passenger door open. Eddie had been in a trance-like state for a minute or more and his parents were already on their way to the office.

"Sorry, Mr Jones. I'm just coming."

Eddie seemed to be more cheerful on the way back to Fenton in the Hillman Minx; it had been a new twist to find the postcard still in his pocket and it was exciting. He couldn't wait to tell Len. Reality and fantasy had, once again, become intertwined. However, his active mind was telling him that there could also be a serious and frightening problem with that concept. There might be a possibility that fantasy could take over completely and he would end up in the same world as his dead friend, with no way back. It had nearly done that in Kent. His wanderings were broken by his dad, who said,

"Do you like the car, Eddie?"

"Yes, it's very comfortable in the back – much more room than the old one."

"Good. It'll have to last us a good few years."

"Are you going to let Jenny learn to drive in it, Dad?"

"I don't know yet. Has she said to you that she wants to drive? She never seems to be interested in cars, not since the accident anyway. Now that Gary's got his licence back, there probably isn't the need and not many girls of her age do drive in any case."

"Would you teach her, Dad?"

Fred Compton didn't answer. Eddie's mum did.

"I don't think your dad would be very good with her. She'll have to save for lessons if she wants to learn."

A few minutes later and Fred Compton drove his new car, almost proudly, onto the drive at number 38. It was just after four. While his dad pottered about checking out his new possession in more detail, Eddie spent the rest of the afternoon watching Grandstand on television. After tea, he repaired to his bedroom to do some reading and more thinking about the momentous events of that morning. His quiet cogitation was disturbed at a little after six by a knock on his door. After a brief pause while he hid the postcard under the bed covers, he shouted,

"Come in!"

Expecting his mum, who had taken to checking on his welfare at regular intervals since Len's death, he was surprised to see his sister standing timidly in the doorway.

"Can I come in, Eddie?"

"Ye-yes," he stammered. "What's up?"

"I want to talk to you."

Eddie looked nervous and slightly embarrassed at the same time.

"What about, Jenny?"

"About you."

"Me? I'm alright. If Mum's sent you to see how I am coping without Len, I'm fine."

Jenny had already sat on the bed next to her brother.

"Mum doesn't know I've come to talk to you. She and Dad have gone for a ride in the car."

Eddie's embarrassment changed totally to nervousness. His sister only ever talked to him if she either had a favour to ask or she wanted to tease him.

"I've got something to tell you that's been bothering me for ages."

Eddie got more nervous. Jenny continued.

"You remember when I told you about meeting the young sailor on the bus to Hamsden?"

Eddie knew what was coming. He had spent many moments thinking about what his sister had said before when she'd met the sailor. He'd guessed at the time that the sailor had been Len's ghost but had put the incident to the back of his mind and there it had stayed until a little while after his friend's death. He still hadn't mentioned it to Len's ghost. He knew that Jenny had been forewarned of something that would make him sad and in need of her care and love. He'd even thought that he should have told Len about it before he had died, but what could he have said? The sailor hadn't mentioned Len; it could have been anything that would mean the Eddie would need looking after. Jenny was getting impatient while her brother seemed to be in a dream.

"Well, do you remember?"

"Yes, of course I do. What about it?"

"I think the sailor knew that something tragic was going to happen to you, Eddie, and he was warning me about it. Do you think he knew that …?"

"Knew what?"

"Knew that Len was going to die."

Eddie said nothing.

"Well, do you?"

150

"How on earth could he know? He was just a sailor, wasn't he?"

It was Jenny's turn to be silent before she said,

"I think he was more than just a sailor. I think I know who he was, Eddie."

Eddie tried to look surprised.

"Who?"

"Len."

Eddie said nothing. What could he say? He wasn't about to 'spill the beans' on the whole story. He was cautious.

"What makes you think that?"

"Because I think I remembered his voice. It sounded like an older version of your friend. Could it have been a ...?"

"What?"

"A ghost?"

"Do you believe in ghosts, then, Jenny?"

"I'm not sure, but what other explanation could there be? He knew me; he knew I had a brother and he knew that soon you'd need my love and care. If it was Len's ghost, could he have known that he was going to die?"

"You're making several assumptions, Jenny."

"Maybe, but I'm convinced it was Len."

Eddie couldn't hold back any longer.

"I've seen him since his death, you know."

"*Seen* him!?"

Eddie hesitated. Had he said too much? He qualified his statement.

"In my dreams, I suppose. I can sense also him during the day sometimes. I talk to him."

"Does he talk to you?"

"I'm not sure. Maybe I pretend that he does. Have you seen him or the sailor since?"

"No, I don't think so. I just feel …."

"Feel what?"

"I just feel maybe I could have done something or told someone, other than you – Mum, perhaps."

"When did you think or know that it was Len? Before or after he died?"

"Oh, well after. Maybe only in the last week or so."

"So, what could you have done? You didn't even have a connection to Len before he died. No one knew what was going to happen – only God."

Eddie tried to forget that he had more or less guessed that Jenny's sailor had been Len's ghost, almost from the moment she had first told him, but nothing had ever suggested itself to him that Len was going to die soon afterwards. The ghost had only made reference to Eddie himself. Jenny went on.

"Do you believe in God, then, Eddie?"

"Yes, I do. Do you?

"I'm not sure, Eddie. If there was a God, how can he let all the sufferings in the world go on?"

Eddie said nothing. He didn't feel like debating such issues with his sister.

"I don't know. Have you told anyone else about your thoughts, Jenny?"

"No. Do you think I should?"

"No. We ought to keep it a secret just between ourselves. Nothing can be changed."

"I suppose you're right. Thanks for listening; at least I don't feel guilty anymore. Nobody could have foreseen Len's tragic death, could they?"

Eddie was about to say, 'God could', but he thought better of it.

Jenny leant across the bed and planted a light kiss on his forehead. He breathed an inward sigh of relief. It was their secret.

15

An Old Friend

The following day, Sunday, Eddie was persuaded to attend morning service at St Andrew's; his discussion with Jenny had provided the motivation and impetus to return to thoughts of God and religion. He'd known for a long time that despite his interest in scientific rigour, other powers existed which were beyond man's understanding. Recent events had only served to confirm this belief – ghosts could not be man-made.

The Reverend Henry Weaver was his usual thought-provoking self and Eddie found himself in his element when he discovered that the sermon for the day was concerned with the afterlife. Eddie had been acquainted with the Christian message for years, without really taking much interest in what it meant for him. He really could not understand that there had to be only one way to salvation and heaven, whatever and wherever that was. Just because someone was born in a non-Christian country should not mean that they were doomed to hell and damnation. It wasn't their fault that they would never be taught or discover about Christianity. What had happened recently had convinced Eddie that the important thing was to have a belief in God and to trust that his greater power could solve any problem, as long as you put your trust in him. Admitting this to oneself, Eddie believed, was the universal solution to personal contentment and salvation. The Reverend Weaver seemed to have elements of this in his sermon that Sunday morning and Eddie felt comfortable in the knowledge that a learned minister of the cloth concurred with his own beliefs. Though he'd never spoken personally to St Andrew's respected vicar before, Eddie decided to ask him a question as the Comptons left church. His parents had gone on ahead as he paused to shake the Reverend Weaver's hand.

"Can I ask you something, Reverend Weaver?"

"Of course you can, Eddie. What's on your mind?"

Eddie was straight to the point with the innocence of youth.

"Are there such things as ghosts?"

"Ghosts?"

"Yes."

"Well now, that's an interesting question, my boy. Why do you ask?"

"No particular reason; I just wondered."

Henry Weaver smiled. He thought he knew why Eddie had asked the question.

"It couldn't have something to do with your recently departed friend, could it?"

Eddie looked a little embarrassed.

"Maybe – it would be nice to see him again."

"Yes, it would and you will one day, Eddie, when we return to our maker."

"I know, but is it possible to see people who have died before then, while we're still alive?"

The Reverend Weaver paused before he answered.

"I don't know, Eddie. What do you think?"

Eddie was mature enough not to reply with, 'You're the one who should know, vicar', and said instead,

"I suppose God can do anything and if he wants us to see people who are already dead, then, yes, I believe it's possible."

"I think you've answered your question. With God, all things are possible as long as we believe."

It was clear to Henry Weaver that Eddie had another question and he asked,

"Something else troubling you?"

After a few seconds, Eddie responded with,

"Can ghosts appear only to some people and not to others?"

"Anything is possible with God, Eddie."

Eddie smiled. 'If only you knew, vicar', he thought.

Fred and Ann Compton had already reached the Red Lion by the time Eddie had finished his extended conversation with Reverend Weaver. The Comptons always called in for a quick drink before Sunday lunch while their son often wandered slowly through town window-shopping. Eddie, for once, decided to take a detour down Mill Road instead of going straight back up the High Street; something he hadn't done for many months, indeed, not since Mr George Canter had owned the junk shop there. Watson's Electrical had replaced it and so it was with some surprise that Eddie discovered the shop open. Paul Watson never opened on a Sunday – he wasn't allowed to by law and he certainly wasn't supposed to trade. Eddie peered in through the window; no lights were on and there didn't seem to be anyone in the shop. Eddie pushed on the open door and went in.

"Come in, my boy. What can I do for you?"

Eddie froze. He hadn't heard that voice in over two years but he had recognised it immediately. He looked around nervously but there was no one to be seen. It was his mind playing tricks again and now he was hearing voices in his head.

"How have you been, Eddie?"

George Canter's voice was coming from behind the counter. Eddie stared at the spot straining his eyes to see if he could make out the source of the phantom sound. The shop had gone suddenly dark.

"Wait a minute, Eddie."

Eddie waited. The shop was now pitch black, making the daylight outside seem unreal. A minute passed with Eddie in complete darkness and silence, broken only by his own shallow breathing and loud heartbeat. A bright light suddenly flashed in front of him causing him to blink and jerk his head back violently. The temporary blindness took a few seconds to wear off and afterwards Eddie knew what he would see. There in front of him, less than four feet away, stood a smiling George Canter.

"Hello, Eddie."

Eddie opened his mouth but no words came out, just an incomprehensible groan.

"Yes, Eddie, it *is* me. I've been waiting for you. I just knew you would come today," said George.

"But what are you doing here? Are you...?"

"Dead?"

"Ye-ye-yes."

"Of course I am, Eddie."

"But how did you get here?"

"Oh Eddie, have you not seen some of my friends already?"

"Your friends?"

"My fellow ghosts. I thought you'd be ready to see me by now and wouldn't be too frightened or dismiss my visit as all in your mind."

Eddie was stunned again into silence. George continued.

"I've seen Len, Eddie, and Mr Grant who owned the shop at the top of Steep Hill – he likes to stay out near Linham where he passed away."

"Where did you see Len?" asked Eddie excitedly.

"He was wandering along the beach earlier this morning."

"Did he see you?"

"No, he seemed to vanish when I got close. I already knew he was dead, but God obviously didn't want us to meet just yet."

Eddie was longing to ask George how he himself had died but couldn't seem to phrase the right question. He managed instead,

"How did you know Len had died?"

"God told me about the car crash, Eddie. You didn't see me but I was at the funeral."

"I miss Len, George."

"I know you do, Eddie, but he will still come and see you whenever he's allowed, you know."

"I suppose so, it's just that...."

"What?"

"It's just that I wish sometimes I could join him."

"What, on a permanent basis?"

Eddie managed a weak grin.

"No, but just whenever I wanted to, like we always used to. I wish I could go to him for advice or just be able to talk to him."

"You will one day," said George with a soft smile. "But you can't go just yet, my boy; you've got your whole life ahead of you."

"So had Len."

"Tragic accidents happen, I'm afraid and there's nothing anyone can do about them. Only God can protect us if we believe, Eddie, and even then he allows chance to play its part in the tapestry of life."

"Do you think that Len was meant to die, then?"

"I don't know, Eddie. Was Aloyisious St John Grant meant to die in the train crash? That was just another tragic and, perhaps, unavoidable accident."

"Have you spoken to Ally – I mean, Mr Grant?"

"Just once this summer when I was allowed to come to Fenton-on-Sea for the first time since I'd left. He told me he liked to walk in the country lanes near Linham and that's what did whenever it was possible."

"Len and I saw him, George – not long after the train crash in the summer of that year. He was dressed in clothes from the early part of the century."

"You and Len were being prepared, I suspect, for you both to be able to cope with Len's tragic death."

Eddie paused. The time had come to ask the difficult question.

"George?"

"Yes? You want to know how I died, I suppose."

"Only if you want to tell me."

George spent a few minutes telling Eddie of the new life he made for himself in the Polish city of Bialystok where he had been born. He had become an antique dealer and had nearly completed his first year of training to become a part-time Rabbi at the new synagogue in the city. Then tragedy had struck. Many years of heavy drinking had caused irreparable damage to his liver and the end had been mercifully quick; just a matter of months culminating in his demise just over a year previously. Eddie listened with sadness until, when George had finished, his melancholy was relieved by his ghost saying,

"Don't be sad, Eddie; I've never felt better or more content. I've seen my parents and my sister and I have made my peace with them and with many of my Jewish friends who died in the holocaust and the burning of The Great Synagogue in Bialystok."

Eddie was about to recount some of the adventures that he and Len had been on since George had left England to go back to Poland, but it was clear that his old friend was becoming tired.

"I'll have to go now, Eddie, but I'll see you again. I will look out for you and try to make sure you don't come to any harm. Goodbye."

"Goodbye, George," replied Eddie but he found himself talking to thin air. George Canter had gone, but another voice echoed in Eddie's head.

"What do you think you are doing, Eddie Compton?"

Eddie spun round to find Mr Paul Watson, owner of Watson's Electrical standing in front of him. He was not best pleased.

"Oh, oh, the door was open, Mr Watson so I thought you …."

"Was it, young man? That still does not give you the right just to walk in, and you know I don't sell anything on a Sunday."

"No, I'm sorry, sir. I was only looking. I thought I could see someone through the window but it must have been a trick of the light."

"Trick of the light, eh? Are you sure you weren't trying to pinch something."

Eddie looked nervous.

"Oh no, Mr Watson – I would never steal anything. I've just come from church with my mum and dad. Honestly."

Mr Watson seemed satisfied and he said,

"I only came to do some stocktaking and then for a pint. I must have forgotten to lock up behind me. It was lucky I came back for something or the shop would have been open until tomorrow morning. Actually, Eddie, I've just left your mum and dad in the Red Lion, so that checks out part of your story but you shouldn't go into private premises, open or not. Now get off home before I change my mind."

"Yes, Mr Watson."

With that, Eddie made his way out of the shop while Mr Watson disappeared into the stockroom at the back.

Eddie's mum and dad were understandably curious when he arrived home almost at the same time as they did, given that they had been in the Red Lion for over forty minutes.

"How come it's taken you until now to get home?" asked Fred Compton as Eddie joined his parents at the front gate.

"Went for a walk along the beach and then looked in a few shops."

Eddie's mum and dad seemed to accept their son's answer. They knew he often wandered off to be by himself and after a knowing look from Eddie's mum, they made their way up the front path and into the house. Once inside, it was clear that Jenny was not at home, even though her mother had left her in charge of the roast dinner. Ann Compton found a scribbled note on the kitchen table.

'Had to go out. Won't be long. I've done all the vegetables and turned the oven off.

> *Love Jenny'.*

Eddie's mum was clearly puzzled.

"I wonder what's happened. Why would she go out on a Sunday morning? Gary's away for the weekend on a fire training exercise."

"That *is* odd," said Eddie's dad, "but I'm hungry and want my dinner. I hope it's not burnt."

The three Comptons had just sat down to their roast lamb dinner when the front door was heard opening and Jenny rushed into the dining room.

"Sorry I'm late. I had to do some emergency babysitting for a friend."

"What friend, dear?" asked Jenny's mum.

"Carole Wilson was looking after her brother Tommy until her mum got back from Hamsden and she had to go out. She phoned me to see if I would babysit Tommy for an hour while she went to see her boyfriend."

Eddie's mum seemed satisfied but Eddie himself knew his sister was lying. He would ask Jenny later where she had been. There was something about her demeanour, and the vague wink she'd given him when giving her explanation, which suggested her absence might have something to do with their discussion of the previous day.

This time it was Eddie who knocked on his sister's bedroom door later that afternoon. He rarely, if ever, went into Jenny's 'boudoir', as he called it. At first, his sister didn't acknowledge Eddie's quiet tapping until his persistence paid off.

"Yes, who is it?"

"Me, you dumb blond. Who did you think it was – Elvis?"

Jenny opened her door about a quarter.

"What do you want?"

"To talk."

The door opened to its full extent and Eddie walked in and sat on his sister's dressing table chair. Jenny had returned to her position propped up on her bed. Magazines lay scattered beside her and she looked as though she had been expecting her brother. Eddie was straight to the point.

"Where did you really go this morning, Jenny? Carole Wilson doesn't have a brother and you know it."

"So why didn't you give me away at lunchtime?"

"Because you winked."

Jenny leant forward on the bed and fixed her gaze on Eddie.

"I think I've seen another ghost."

"Where?"

"Here – he came to the house this morning just before twelve."

"Why did you think it was a ghost?" asked Eddie with disbelief echoing in his question.

"I'll tell you in a minute."

"Did you recognise him?"

"I think so. It looked like…."

"Who, Jenny?"

"That man who used to own the junk shop in Mill Road – Mr Canter, I think he was called. Mum said he'd gone to Poland a couple of years ago, so that's why I started thinking that he might be a ghost."

"What did he want?"

"You."

"Me?"

"Yes, he asked me where you were and I told him you'd gone to St Andrew's with Mum and Dad."

"What did he say then?"

"He just thanked me and put his hand on my arm, but …."

Eddie guessed what Jenny would say next and he helped her out.

"But you couldn't feel his touch and his hand went right through your arm."

"Yes. It was really spooky, Eddie. I was touched by a ghost."

"What did he do then?"

"He just turned round and walked down the front path. I lost sight of him when he'd gone out of the front gate. What does it all mean, Eddie?"

"I don't know."

Jenny looked close to tears and after a pause she said,

"He said something else, Eddie."

"What?"

"He said that I should keep a close eye on you and to try to make sure that you didn't get into any trouble. It felt like when Len's ghost warned me that you would need my care."

"Maybe your imagination ran away with you when you thought you were talking to a ghost," said Eddie. "Maybe you were just reminded of what Len had said because Mr Canter appeared to be that ghost. Remember, Jenny, ghosts aren't real."

"He seemed real enough to me, Eddie. Am I going mad?"

"No, you're not going mad but it still doesn't answer my question as to why you went out."

"I tried to follow him."

"And?"

"When I got to the gate I thought I could still see him in the distance and he appeared to be waiting near the end of the road. It had taken me a few minutes to write the note and get some clothes on so he must have been there a while. By the time I got to South Road he had moved again and I assumed he'd gone down the High Street. I eventually spotted him near the turning to Mill Road but when I got there he had disappeared. I wandered about for a while looking for him by which time it was getting late and I returned here."

Eddie looked pensive. He had another question.

"What time did the man you thought was Mr Canter, disappear?"

"About twenty past twelve."

'Just about the time that I left church', thought Eddie. His sister's story began to make sense. He debated whether to tell his sister of his own ghostly meeting, but decided against it. Jenny had had enough of phantom strangers for one day. Fear was etched all over her face. Their shared secret was becoming more difficult to keep too.

Later that evening Eddie began to feel sad for his old friend, George Canter. Why did have to die when he was such a nice and generous man? Eddie consoled himself in the knowledge that George had appeared to be content and had found peace in death. With Len's passing as well, death did not seem such a bad thing after all. At least two people had an air of happiness that they had not possessed when they had been alive.

16

Nightmares

Eddie spent much of that Sunday evening in his room, reading and thinking about the conversation with his sister. He realised that she had experienced as startling an encounter as he had done, and though nothing really extraordinary had happened to Jenny, she seemed fairly convinced that it hadn't been just a figment of her imagination. He knew that his sister wouldn't say anything to anyone else, for fear of being ridiculed and, perhaps with time, she would forget the whole thing. What had George meant by his warning though? In the end Eddie decided that it had probably been a natural thing for him to say because Len had died and George was concerned for Eddie's well-being in the future. He was comforted, however, by the fact that George had seen Len that morning, but disappointed that his best friend hadn't come to see him as well. By the time Eddie went to sleep, he had reconciled this omission with the knowledge that Len was not in control of his visits to the real world.

It was a gloriously sunny late autumn day and Eddie was gazing wistfully out of the window of Room 46 where he was listening to Mr Green drone on about a particularly difficult scene from the end of Henry the Fifth.

"And what does the phrase, '*stops the mouth of all find-faults*', mean, Mr Compton?"

"Sorry, sir?"

"*Stops the mouth of all find-faults*. What does Shakespeare mean, please?"

"I don't know, sir."

"Well hazard a guess, please."

Eddie tried to locate the phrase in his copy of the play but only a nudge from Sally Barber, indicating the turn of a page, helped him find the right place. Mr Green was getting angry.

"Well?"

Suddenly Eddie's world was plunged into darkness and somewhere in the distance he heard,

"*I'm waiting.*"

Eddie's mouth wouldn't open; he was terrified, and then, in the gloom, he could just make out Mr Green bearing down on him with an ugly-looking cane in his hand. The cane was raised above his head and descended quickly in an arc with a frightening swish. Eddie ducked and fell off his seat onto the floor. Normal light returned. He heard raucous laughter from all around his prostrate position. Mr Green was still standing, arms folded, at the front of the classroom.

"You will see me at the end of the lesson, boy. Now return to your seat and sit on it properly. I'll show you later what I do with boys who don't pay attention and fall of their chairs for no apparent reason."

After the lesson had finished, Mr Green told Eddie to go and wait for him in the assembly hall where his punishment would be meted out. English, being the last class of the day meant the main hall would be empty. It was with some apprehension that Eddie walked across the upper quadrangle and into the barely-lit hall. What punishment had Mr Green in mind that entailed the use of the assembly hall? Was Eddie about to be made to read out the whole of the last act of Henry the Fifth from the stage? He opened a side door and walked into the auditorium. It was empty; not even a cleaner in sight. Eddie climbed up the three steps onto the main stage. He'd rarely been in such an elevated position during his time thus far at Fenton Grammar School. He walked to the lectern and pretended to be making a speech as if he were the Headmaster, Mr D J Hempsall. A familiar voice sounded out from somewhere behind him.

"Now we will see how we make boys like you learn to pay attention, Compton."

Eddie looked round. There was no one there. The voice continued.

"Go to the lectern, place your arms on it and make a straight back with your legs apart. You're going to feel a little pain in your backside in a minute."

Eddie had never been caned before and he was scared. Could Mr Green do this? Wasn't Mr Hempsall the only one allowed to issue such punishment? How hard would he be hit? He put himself in the position as directed by his English teacher.

"Good, now wait while I fetch my special thin cane with the metal end."

Eddie waited and he began to tremble with real fear. This sounded as if he was going to suffer some serious pain. Surely a teacher could not do this. He would show his parents the weals. It was getting darker outside and his back and sides were beginning to ache. Where was Mr Green? He glanced at his watch – it was twenty to five. How long had he been standing in this awkward position? Twenty, thirty minutes? Suddenly, he heard footsteps echo on the wooden floor behind him, to be followed by the sound of a cane being swished through the air. He began to cry. He'd never ever been this scared before. He could feel Mr Green's hot breath on his neck. His English master put his face against Eddie's ear and said,

"Now it won't hurt too much provided you keep absolutely still and don't turn round. Prepare yourself. One, two, three ...."

Eddie braced himself for the first blow. He heard the cane make its arc through the air. He screamed.

"No, oh please, no!"

The cane must have missed because Eddie felt no pain. He waited for a second attempt but now there was silence apart from his own heavy breathing and intermittent sobbing. He tried to turn round but his body was rigid with fear and seemed to be locked in position. Eventually, he prised himself upright and turned his head. Mr Green was nowhere to be seen. The voice echoed throughout the hall.

"*Hope that scared you, Mr Compton. Please pay attention in my lessons in future. Now, go home.*"

After a few moments while he regained his composure, Eddie made to leave the stage to go home. He decided there and then that he wouldn't mention Mr Green's sick idea of a school punishment to his parents. His dad would only have said that he deserved it and what were a few tears to complain about anyway? Eddie knew that what Mr Green had done was not ethical, but he had learned his lesson – he would pay attention from then on. He jumped down off the stage and made for the door. It was locked. He walked to the back of the hall and attempted to open both of the only other two exit doors. They were securely locked. The school assembly hall had windows but they were high up and all looked tightly closed. He looked at his watch – it was ten past five, but it seemed later judging by the darkness of the sky which was visible through the windows above him. He shouted,

"Help! Help! I'm locked in!"

Surely not everyone had gone home. He began to panic as he ran to the first door again and shook it violently. Then the horrible thought took hold – he could be locked in until morning when the cleaners would be the first to open up the hall. His parents would be worried by now. Would they think to come and find him? How would they know where he was anyway? Would they know who to contact? Eddie sat down on a chair and cried out loud,

"Please, someone help me! Help my mum and dad find me."

Minutes passed and it had become almost pitch black in the hall. His panic got worse as he put his head in his hands. He tried shouting again.

"Oh God, please help me! Please, please help me!"

"It's alright, Eddie, just wake up."

Light beamed into his face as he opened his eyes. He was in bed and his mum, in her nightdress, was standing over him. It had been a nightmare. He sat up with a jerk and wiped the cold sweat from his brow. His mum sat down on his bed and said soothingly.

"You've had a bad dream, Eddie, that's all. You've been shouting for a few minutes and woke us all up."

"What did I say, Mum?"

"Couldn't hear or understand most of it, but you were obviously in some sort of trouble. What was the nightmare all about?"

Eddie tried to recall his dream but nothing would come back – just a vague impression that it had been something to do with school. By morning he would discover that even that fleeting memory would have gone from his head. He would remember later, however, that he had had a bad nightmare that seemed to have drained the very life out of him. He hoped he would not have another one very quickly. His mother left the landing light on for the rest of that night and his bedroom door ajar. The emotional exhaustion eventually forced him into a dreamless sleep until morning.

All was not well for Eddie at school the next day. He felt lethargic and he was troubled by the restless night he'd had – he still had no memory of the bad dream. He couldn't concentrate on his favourite subjects, Maths and Science, in the morning and, by the afternoon English lesson with Mr Green, all he really wanted to do was to go home and sleep. Something about his English master's demeanour told him that he was not pleased with his latest essay on Henry the Fifth that was due back that afternoon. Mr Green took great pleasure in handing individual pieces of work back to his pupils with the inevitable cutting remark even if the recipient had produced a superb essay. Eddie didn't have to wait long; his essay was the fourth to be discussed.

"Well, Compo, I'm afraid you have excelled yourself this time. It certainly isn't your usual rubbish."

Eddie gave a relieved smile.

"No, Mr Compton, it's better than that. This time it's utter and complete rubbish. Well done! You'd better see me at the end of the lesson."

Mr Green flung Eddie's exercise book onto his desk but he hardly noticed it. His memory had been jogged as unrelated pieces of his nightmare began to come back to him. He had been in Mr Green's lesson then, he was sure of it. But what had happened? He knew it hadn't been pleasant but he just couldn't remember the detail. He had an hour to wait for his punishment for the terrible essay. He was tired and wanted to get home to sleep. Fortunately, Mr Green left him well alone for the rest of the lesson, a good part of which was spent on the other twenty-three recipients of his English teacher's caustic remarks. His own essay appeared to have been by far the worst.

At four o'clock by his watch, Eddie found himself once again standing on the assembly hall stage; though this time it had to be for real. Mr Green had told him to go straight to the hall after the end of his lesson. He had remembered most of his nightmare from the moment he had entered the poorly-lit building. The situation presented to him, however, was far worse than his dream. Not only did he know what was coming, but he also knew that this time there would be no rescue by his mum out of the nightmare. He had remembered from the previous night that he had been locked in the hall and, though the memory was vague, he recalled being in a blind panic and shouting for help. Panic began to set in again as he sat forlornly on the sole chair on the stage. Frightening thoughts entered his brain. Was his current situation real or had he been plunged into another nightmare? How could he tell reality from fantasy?

Half an hour passed by his watch and Mr Green did not appear. Was this to be his punishment – a silent detention? After another five minutes, he decided that he had enough; this wasn't fair. Half expecting the door to be locked he made for the exit. To his relief it opened easily and he emerged into the twilight. Immediately his feet sank into something soft and cold. It had been snowing and heavily. But it was only early November and, though it had been a cold day, snow was definitely not forecast. Eddie trudged forward and, once his eyes had adjusted to the pure-white surroundings, he looked around himself. Terror and panic set in simultaneously. He wasn't in the upper quadrangle or anything like it. He looked back over his shoulder. The assembly hall had disappeared! Whichever way he looked, the landscape was an unbroken panorama of white. He was in an enormous flat snowfield that stretched to the horizon in all directions. No landmarks were visible and it was unbearably cold; he had on only his normal school uniform with an extra pullover for the chill autumn day. The frightening thoughts returned. This wasn't a dream; he had been at school, hadn't he? He'd been plunged into a fantasy world and there was no Len to help him. This was not good. Nightmares when sleeping were bad enough, and to be expected occasionally, but this was different. How could you have a nightmare during the day? What should he do? He tried to pinch himself on his cheek to see if he himself was real, but he couldn't make his fingers close; they were already too cold. He looked at his watch – it was a quarter past three. He looked again. That could not be right; it had already been at least half past four when he had left the hall. He edged forward in the snow; it was getting very deep, deeper than any snow he'd ever known. It was above his knees and soon he could hardly lift his legs to move. He was stranded and seemed to be sinking, sinking, sinking ….

"Wake up, Eddie. Time to go home."

A familiar girl's voice sounded in the icy air around his head. He felt a light touch on his left arm. A deeper voice spoke.

"What is it, Sally?"

"It's Eddie Compton, Mr Green; he's fallen asleep."

Footsteps on a wooden floor. Chairs being moved loudly. Chattering voices.

"Asleep, eh? I'll give him, asleep!"

"I don't think he's well, sir. He looked very pale when he came into the lesson."

A gentle shake of his right shoulder. He felt warmer and safe.

"What's happened?" asked Eddie as his head jolted upright from its position lying on the desk.

"You fell asleep," said Sally Barber.

"Are you alright, Compton?" asked Mr Green with surprising sympathy in his voice. Eddie looked around him. He was back in Room 46 and his classmates had all left to go home. Only Sally and Mr Green remained and both had anxious looks on their faces.

"I'm O.K., sir. Must have fallen asleep. I'm sorry, sir."

"That's alright, young man. I bet you've got a touch of flu or something. Better get your mum to take you to the doctors. Will you be alright to get home on your own?"

"Yes, sir, I'll be fine. I didn't sleep well last night, that's all."

Sally Barber walked part of the way home with Eddie and, after she had left him at the entrance to Fir Tree Close, he dawdled while he pondered the afternoon's event. One horrible thought kept coming back to him: 'How could he ever feel safe in going to sleep again, whether at home in his bed or anywhere else, especially when the nightmares had seemed as real as reality itself'?

17
Déjà Vu

Eddie got very little sleep that Monday night and by the morning he was looking almost as pale as his clean white shirt. He had tried desperately to keep his eyes closed but even with the light on, it was well after two before he entered the dubious sanctuary of oblivion. His mother showed her concern at breakfast.

"You look awful, Eddie. Do you feel ill?"

"No, Mum, I'm just very tired. I didn't get much sleep again."

"Why? Is something troubling you?"

"I don't know, Mum," he lied. "Bad dreams I suppose."

"Well you're in no fit state to go to school. I'll ring and say you're sick."

"No, Mum, I'll be fine. I've nothing to do at home."

"Precisely, that's just what you need – a day of complete rest. I'll make an appointment at the doctors for some sleeping tablets or something. It's probably just a growing phase. You're not still fretting about Len, are you? I know you miss him, but you've got to move on, Eddie. Haven't you got other friends at school?"

"A few, Mum, and I'm not really missing Len now. I'd rather go to school; I'd be so bored at home. It's only tiredness."

"Well alright, then, but I will make an appointment for you to see Dr Rees and we'll see what he says."

"O.K., but only as long as I can go on my own; I'm fifteen next year and make the appointment for after school, Mum."

"Just as you like, but you might have to wait a few days."

"No problem, I'll have got some sleep by then."

Eddie thought afterwards that that intention might prove difficult unless he could talk to Len or even another friendly ghost, like George Canter. They were bound to know what was happening to him. Len, for one, had always solved his non-academic problems in the past and he couldn't discuss his fears within anyone else, least of all his parents.

All the fourth year at Fenton Grammar had an afternoon of House football on the Tuesday afternoon, but Eddie had been excused; his mother had insisted on writing a note because of his lack of sleep. Along with three others he had been despatched to the library to do private study. Together with a few sixth-formers, who hadn't got permission to go home early, there were only about a dozen students occupying the school's second largest room. Its beamed and sloping ceiling together with some internal buttresses allowed some occupants to be hidden from view of anyone else in the library. Eddie found one such space at the far end and settled down to write up some science experiments. He had a science fiction novel in reserve should he finish the school work. The library was uncomfortably warm and despite his previous fears, Eddie felt safe and was soon fast asleep with his head resting on a pile of books, strategically placed on the table in front of him.

Len had had a feeling for some time that his best friend was in need of his company and counsel. He had been provided with a brief visit to the beach at Fenton-on-Sea just two days previously and had walked for about half a mile wondering why he was there and what he was supposed to do. Memories of George Canter had come back to him for a while that Sunday morning, but then all at once he had gone into his normal ghostly sleep and oblivion. He now found himself outside the familiar library at his old school. The clock outside read twenty past three. In his ghostly disguise, Len had quickly learnt that he didn't need to do mundane things like open doors and he glided quietly and unnoticed 'through' the library wall.

Eddie had slept soundly for about fifty minutes when he first began to dream. He could hear a familiar voice which sounded as though it was coming from a long way off.

"*Wake up, old son.*"

'I'm not asleep', thought Eddie as a cool waft of air blew on his neck. He tried to form the words with his mouth but his lips were glued together.

"*Your old friend Len is here. Now open your eyes.*"

This time an icy draught blew directly into Eddie's face causing his eyelids to flutter.

"*That's it, Captain. Time to come back to the land of the living.*"

Eddie's head dislodged itself from his pile of books and only his body's natural instinct to protect itself saved his face from dropping onto the table. He sat up with a jerk.

"Wha-what!" he muttered blindly.

A chorus of '*Shut ups*' broke out from several sixth-formers as Eddie groaned some more.

"It's me, Eddie."

Eddie's eyes at last opened fully and he focused on his best friend.

"Len? How ...?"

"Shh! I'll do the talking. Only you will be able to hear. Just nod whenever you need to."

Eddie nodded. Aaron Johnson of 6Sc2 smirked at the fourth-former's strange behaviour but put it down to the natural emergence from his deep sleep. Len continued to address Eddie from his position standing directly in front of the table.

"I want to talk to you again, Eddie. I've things to tell you and I suspect you have things to tell me, eh?"

Eddie nodded.

"I have one or two surprises for you and an explanation of some things you and I have seen in the past – O.K?

Eddie nodded. Len leant forward and looked directly into his friend's eyes holding his gaze.

"Go to Freeman Street next Saturday."

Eddie hesitated slightly while he took in this simple but direct instruction. He nodded. Len disappeared immediately in a blur. Len's voice, however, continued with a qualification of his order.

"Go and watch the game from behind the goal in the North Stand."

Eddie nodded involuntarily at the empty space in front of him. The bell for end of afternoon school rang loudly.

It wasn't until the following evening that Eddie's dad brought home the Wednesday edition of the Hamsden Daily Star, which always featured Saturday's forthcoming game. Fred Compton took his usual leisurely time in perusing the paper and Eddie had to wait patiently for him to finish. Having finished his second cup of tea after his dinner, Eddie's dad put the Daily Star down on the table beside him.

"Can I have a look, Dad?" asked Eddie politely.

"Of course you can, son, but there's nothing much in it; just more and more adverts."

Eddie took the paper up to his bedroom trying not to arouse his parents' suspicion. They seemed to be discussing plans for that Christmas including a possible invite to Martha Wilby for whom it would be the first such occasion without her son and husband. As he climbed the stairs he could just hear his father saying,

"Well, she might want to be on her own, love."

From a previous visit to the garden at number 23 The Park, Eddie had his suspicions that Aunty Martha would not be on her own.

Details of Saturday's game were always contained on the inside back page and Eddie turned there immediately. He looked at the headline:

'TOWN TAKE ON NEW BOYS BRADFIELD ORIENT'.

Eddie started reading. Bradfield Orient had been promoted from the Fourth Division at the start of the current season after a runaway success as champions. Eddie knew little about them except that they were based in south-east London not far from first division Crystal Palace who often supplied them with young players. The game was to be played at Freeman Street as Len had indicated – kick-off, three o'clock. Eddie had in the back of his mind how and in what form he would meet Len ever since his friend's instruction in the library. He couldn't wait for Saturday to come round. For each of the three nights until the big day, Eddie enjoyed a dreamless and reinvigorating sleep; his colour improved to such an extent that his mother cancelled the doctor's appointment arranged for the following Monday.

By Saturday, the 13th of November, the weather had turned cold with early morning frosts. Though the morning was dull and overcast, by the time Eddie caught the half past one train to Hamsden, it had brightened considerably with a late autumn sun trying to peep through the clouds. Eddie had to stand for most of the way; the four-carriage diesel railcar was packed with both football fans and early Christmas shoppers. No one of any significance, human or otherwise, got on at Linham Junction and the train arrived safely at Hamsden station at four minutes past two. Eddie spotted several of his fellow fourth years as he walked along the platform to the station exit that opened onto the broad thoroughfare that led down to Freeman Street.

"Going to the game, Compton?" shouted Bob Felton from about five yards behind him. "Want to come with us?"

Robert Felton was an inferior version of his best friend, Len – blond-haired, sporty and the new captain of the Under 15's football team. He was, however, arrogant and had a reputation as a bully, particularly of those either younger or smaller than himself. Bob Felton was the last person Eddie wanted to be seen with especially as he had private business to attend to as well. Eddie turned bravely to face his questioner.

"No thanks, I'm meeting someone in the North Stand."

Bob threw back his blond head and laughed. The North Stand was for cissies and families and definitely not for the budding hooligans that he and his friends were destined to become.

"Suit yourself, but don't talk to any strange men, Compton!"

The bully and his loyal following of three associates hurried past Eddie, each giving him a not so friendly push against his shoulder. One whispered in Eddie's ear,

"Take care, Edwina and beware of the bogeyman."

Eddie laughed inwardly at his moronic peers and he walked slowly so that the gang of four would be as far away as possible before he reached the ground. Leonard Wilby would have made mincemeat of young Robert Felton, thought Eddie, as he strolled down Station Road. Len had always despised the bully when he had been at Fenton Grammar. It took Eddie nearly twenty minutes to dawdle the half mile and he arrived at the North Stand entrance at just before half past two. The North

Stand was pricier to get into than most other parts of Freeman Street but, at least, he would be unlikely to meet any other grammar school pupils there. Len had chosen well.

It was clear to Eddie, as soon as he got inside the ground that the crowd was going to be well short of full capacity and he was able to acquire a good position behind the goal with ease. Christmas shopping was obviously the main priority for many of Town's normal fans. It was not surprising given their lowly league position; a serious leg injury to their star forward, Johnny McBride, had not helped in their quest for goals and their leaky defence meant they were haunted by fears of relegation to the fourth tier of the football league. For their part, Bradfield Orient had brought a sizeable contingent of travelling fans who, to Eddie's dismay, had been allocated a large section of the North Stand directly behind him. The Orient had continued the success of the previous campaign and was currently lying in third position. It was going to be a hard game for the lowly Town.

Eddie had bought a match programme for sixpence but it wasn't until he had established his position a few rows back from the concrete retaining wall that he decided to open it and look at the teams. He already knew what he would find. There on the opposition team sheet, playing at inside right, was one L. Wilton.

At five to the hour precisely, the visitors took the field first and Eddie strained his eyes to pick out their number eight. He looked younger than when Eddie had last seen him playing for Spurs in the pre-season friendly. He appeared to be barely out of school and this was soon confirmed by an overheard conversation between two of the visiting supporters.

"That boy Wilton is playing again today."

"He looks a good prospect for a seventeen-year-old."

"Yeah, he came from Palace's youth team that reached the youth semi-final last year."

It wasn't until the second half that the visitors were kicking towards the North Stand goal after establishing a two-goal lead, courtesy of two assists from the young Wilton. The déjà vu moment happened in the sixty-third minute with one subtle difference. This time the young inside forward picked up the ball on the half-way line and strode purposefully forward delicately avoiding desperate tackles. Reaching the edge of the penalty area, he drove a low rasping shot which skimmed the left-hand goalpost and straight into Eddie's waiting arms. Several of the crowd in his vicinity shouted,

"Well caught, son!"

"Give us the ball, Captain," said young Wilton.

Eddie moved to the concrete wall and handed the ball back and got just close enough to hear a whispered,

"Go to the players' entrance after the game."

A silver St Christopher glinted in the low afternoon sun.

For the rest of the game Eddie's mind was in turmoil. This could not be possible despite all the other ghostly encounters. The young Orient footballer was *real* and yet he looked and spoke like Len. He wasn't a ghost. It just did not make sense.

At the end of the game, Eddie made his way round to the other side of the ground, joining several other fans seeking autographs from their favourite players. He was filled with apprehension as to whom or what he would find. He didn't have to wait long as the visiting team seemed to be anxious to get back to London where they could celebrate their resounding 4–0 victory. The jubilant Orient side filed onto their waiting coach and Eddie counted each member of the team one by one. Wilton was the last to board, but board he did, without any acknowledgement of Eddie. He thought he overheard the young number eight talking to a fellow player and his voice did not seem so familiar as before. Something about his walk also was different from his best friend's gait. As with the pre-season friendly, he had been confused by the similarity between both players in name and physique. A voice spoke from behind him.

"Good trick, eh, Eddie?"

Eddie turned round and there stood Len grinning from ear to ear. He appeared to be same age as earlier in the week in the school library. Immediately Eddie tried to put his hand on Len's arm and felt just empty space. For the first time ever he was pleased that Len was a ghost!

"How did you do that, Len?"

"It takes a little practice but I've learnt that we ghosts can take on other forms, you know. We can get inside other people's heads and become that person for a short while. Mr Larry Wilton had absolutely no idea that, for a few moments in the second half, he spoke a couple of sentences to a young fourteen-year-old boy. In addition I was able to make you think that it was me. He has gone back to London blissfully unaware of anything unusual."

"But he had a St Christopher round his neck."

Len smiled.

"Are you sure he did? Did you touch it?"

"Well, no, but I saw it."

"No, Eddie – you saw and heard what you were allowed to see and hear. There's a big difference, you know"

Eddie was deep in thought.

"So it was you back in August before you died. You were playing for Spurs' reserves."

Len looked puzzled.

"What do you mean?"

Eddie then described the incident with the Spurs' player called Wilton at the pre-season friendly. It was news to Len and he could only offer one explanation.

"I must have gone back in time and given you a taste of what is possible when you are a ghost."

"Maybe it was a warning that you were going to die. I just assumed that, because you had recently moved, I was missing you and I kept seeing you everywhere I looked. I *wanted* you to be the young Spurs' player."

"Probably so, Eddie. I just know as a ghost I can probably be anyone or anything I want to be and I can go anywhere I choose. Today I was a lower-league footballer. Next time I might be a first division superstar or a brain surgeon or a ...."

"A nuclear scientist?"

18

Invisible and Alone

Len didn't stay much longer with Eddie at Freeman Street; once again his exertions seemed to have exhausted him. He left Eddie with a whispered cryptic comment.

"Green will change to blue. Wait for the sunshine."

Apart from the possible reference to his English teacher, Eddie couldn't really find a satisfactory interpretation for the strange words. It would be another fortnight until an explanation would become apparent.

The days following his visit to Freeman Street were void of any significant dreams at night for Eddie and with proper rest; he did not drift off into sleep during the day either. The weather was typical for November – dull and misty with thick fog at times. The sun was notable by its absence. His English lessons were uneventful and he reached the afternoon of Friday the 26th in relaxed mood as he went to his last class of the week with Mr Green. His academic nemesis was in a good mood for a change, even complimenting Eddie on his recent essay on a poem of Robert Frost.

"A good attempt by you, Mr Compton; quite out of character. Did someone help you with it?"

"No, sir. I like poetry, especially his *Ghost House* poem."

Eddie had found the poem fascinating. Some lines in particular stood out for him:

> '*I know not who these mute folk are ...*'
> '*... And yet, in view of how many things,*
> *As sweet companions as might be had*'.

When he read the first line, it had worried Eddie to begin with. Ghosts were supposed to be silent according to Frost, but then he realised that they *were* silent to all but those they wished to communicate with. The final two lines of the poem gave him great solace – Len was much nicer dead!

Eddie beamed with pride for most of the rest of that English lesson. He couldn't remember a time when an English teacher had given him any praise. The day felt better all round and, even outside through the window of Room 46, he could see a deep yellow sun peeping from behind the clouds against a sky of rich blue. Len's final words at the game came back to Eddie with real meaning. '*Green will change to blue. Wait for the sunshine*'. Something was going to happen very soon.

Eddie was filled with anticipation when he got up on Saturday morning. Fenton-on-Sea awoke to a beautiful day with a golden sun and a clear blue sky; all the ingredients contained in Len's cryptic remark. Something was telling Eddie at breakfast that he needed to be prepared for a complete day out and he organised himself accordingly when his mother asked him about his plans for the day.

"What are you going to do today? You need some fresh air after your recent problems."

"Yes, Mum. I think I'll go to Hamsden for the day. Town are at home this afternoon as well."

Eddie guessed that Len might meet him near the station as he had done before and his plan would cater for that possibility. Len hadn't mentioned any specific meeting place in his strange words. His mum looked pleased that her son was going to spend his Saturday in the way that any normal boy of his age would.

"Good idea, Eddie. Have you got enough money?"

"I will have if Dad gives me this and last week's pocket money," replied Eddie glancing in the direction of his dad who was about to get up from the table to go to work at the station. Fred Compton paused and made great play of digging deep into his trouser pocket as if he had to scrape together his last few pennies to make the required sum. He opened his hand to reveal no more than a few pence and shook his head in resignation. Eddie's head went down in mock sadness to match his dad's pretence of poverty.

"I only get four shillings a week, Dad. Can't you spare it for your favourite son?"

Eddie pretended to sob. His dad reached inside his British Rail jacket and produced his old brown leather wallet from which he extracted a crisp pound note.

"Get me a match programme and it's yours."

Eddie raised his head in a pretence of excitement and said,

"Done. Thanks, Dad."

"That's alright, son. Have a good day and enjoy yourself. It won't be many more months before you will have to work on a Saturday to get your own pocket money."

Eddie didn't tarry outside Fenton station when he went to catch the ten past nine train. He had decided that if Len was to appear he would do so in his own time. Despite his plea of poverty, Eddie had over three pounds in his wallet and pocket; he seemed to spend less without anyone to help him do it on a Saturday. He had enough money to get him a long way by train if need be.

The train was not as packed as that on the Saturday a fortnight previous. It was too early for the football fans and even for all but the most enthusiastic Christmas shoppers. Eddie found a seat in the front carriage with an empty one beside him, just in case .... He settled back and tried to enjoy the ride to Hamsden.

Linham Junction was the first place where he thought his friend might put in an appearance, but no one got on or off and the train progressed as normal towards its destination, reaching Hamsden station at just after a quarter to ten. As he alighted from the train, Eddie pondered his situation. What should he do? He had fully expected that Len would have shown himself by then. It was nearly five hours to the match at Freeman Street and he didn't really have any shopping that he wanted to do. Ten minutes later and he found himself wandering aimlessly among the early morning shoppers in the High Street. He began murmuring to himself.

"Where are you, old boy? Where are you?"

He half expected that his quiet plea would do the trick, but apart from an odd look from a passing shopper, nothing happened. Then he remembered that, on another occasion, he and Len had been transported to Osborne's department store. He headed further up the High Street towards Hamsden's largest shop and, once inside, he made for the same counter in the toy department where the previous rendezvous had taken place. Without trying to look conspicuous he studied the glass-fronted cabinets containing a variety of toys for sale. A familiar voice whispered from behind him.

"You're here again, then, Captain. It's been a while."

Eddie turned to meet his friend who was standing with his usual cheeky grin.

"What have you been up to?" continued Len.

Len looked a little older than when issuing his riddle outside the players' entrance at Freeman Street, but Eddie had begun to realise that he was seeing him so infrequently that he was bound to appear to age between visits. Eddie whispered so no one else should hear, although, fortunately, the only other person in the vicinity was the shop assistant and she was a good twenty feet away.

"Not much since I saw you after the match."

Len seemed to ignore Eddie's reply and, coming right up to him, he asked in a low voice,

"What do you fancy doing?"

"I don't know – I thought you had plans after your riddle about green turning to blue."

Len said nothing. He looked puzzled. Suddenly, in a reversal of roles, another voice entered Eddie's head.

"*Keep away from him, Eddie. Leave him to me.*"

Len continued to stand with a frown on his face. Eddie turned round to face the source of the new voice. Another Len stood less than six feet away and he had a silver St Christopher around his neck. He walked past his open-mouthed friend and said something incomprehensible to the evil ghost who promptly vanished from sight. The real Len returned to Eddie's side and said,

"Let's go somewhere we can talk," and, as if to prove his identity, he continued, "A dull Green day has become a blue day full of sunshine, eh?"

Five minutes late and Eddie had led his friendly ghost to where the High Street began to merge with the more residential area of town. A few hundred yards further on and they were outside the entrance to the War Memorial Gardens. Once inside, they found a wooden bench, conveniently hidden from view of most of the rest of the almost deserted haven of small lawns and shrubberies. Eddie sat down while Len stood in front of him. No one but Eddie would hear what Len was about to say.

"You have to be careful, Eddie. My evil ghost seems to frequent Osborne's on a regular basis. Always ask him only something I would know to check if it's me or not."

"I was just about to, Len. He obviously was unaware of your riddle or even meeting me after the match at Freeman Street."

"Good, but there's another way of knowing."

"How?"

Len pulled his St Christopher forward from his neck.

"Look for this. I'll always wear it from now on, but still be careful because he may get one for himself."

Eddie thought for a moment.

"We need a coded signal, just in case."

"What do you suggest?" asked Len.

"Something from my past that I haven't even told you, in case …."

"In case?"

"In case, as your ghost, he can remember everything that he experienced when he was alive as your evil half."

"What about something that has happened to you after I died?" said Len.

"I think he'd know that as one of your ghosts. He seems to know where I am at times so he's probably been stalking and haunting me without me being aware."

Len appeared to nod his agreement.

"Can you think of something? You used to tell me everything."

"There is something, I think, that I haven't told another living soul."

Len grinned.

"Have you told a dead one, then?"

"Not yet; you'll be the first!"

190

Len's grin got broader.

"Go on, then, tell comrade Len. I promise never to tell anyone, living or dead!"

"I stole something once."

"What?"

"Well, it was before you and your family came to Fenton-on-Sea from London."

Eddie looked guilty as he continued,

"I was about seven and Mum and I were in Woolworth's on a Saturday morning. While she was paying for some sweets and with nobody looking I pinched an extra sweet from the tray on the counter."

"And you're sure no one saw you?"

"Absolutely certain, Len."

"Well? What's the big secret?"

"I'll tell you what kind of sweet it was."

"And?"

"It was a chocolate éclair."

"So that's the signal – chocolate éclair?

"Yes."

Len wasn't totally convinced.

"Only one problem, Captain."

"What's that?"

"My evil ghost is probably listening or can read my mind."

"Got to be worth trying though."

"O.K., Captain," said Len finally.

Eddie stood up from the bench as an elderly couple with a dog appeared to want to sit down. The dog barked loudly at the empty space in front of Eddie and then began to growl menacingly. The pensioners reined it back with suitably corrective words. Eddie made quickly for the exit to the gardens with Len's ghost in tow.

"Animals can sense you," said Eddie as they reached the road.

"They have stronger senses, I suppose," responded Len.

Eddie stopped walking back towards the town centre and, with no one in earshot or sight, said,

"Why have you come back today, Len?"

"Aren't you pleased to see me?"

"Oh yes, and I've had some bad nightmares that I wanted to tell you about anyway."

"I know, Eddie. I sensed you had a rough time with old man Green."

"He's been O.K. with me recently and the nightmares have stopped."

"Good. I did try to haunt the old duffer and give him a taste of his own medicine."

"Wow! You can do that?"

"Sometimes, but only if the power is used for good and not to just gain an advantage over somebody or some thing."

Eddie began walking again and before they reached the busy town centre itself, he began to tell Len about George Canter's death and the meeting with his ghost. As he talked he kept his head down as if looking at the pavement. Len didn't seem to be aware of either event even though George had been only a few yards from him on the morning in question. Len, also, wasn't as sad as Eddie thought he should have been on learning of their special friend's demise.

"Death is only a beginning, Eddie. George is more content now and he has his whole death in front of him," he joked. "Maybe I'll get to see him in the non-flesh."

192

Eddie smiled at his friend's relaxed attitude to the most difficult and frightening subject the human race had to face. He made death seem fun and to be looked forward to!

Len stopped his ghostly walk in a conveniently quiet spot and said,

"I'll tell you why I've really come today."

"Why?"

"I thought you might like a day out. You can choose where you would like to go and I'll see if I can engineer it."

"What – anywhere?"

"Anywhere you like."

"Will you be coming with me?"

"How would you get back without me?"

"True."

Eddie had already been thinking of a possible destination, ever since he knew that Len could transport them across distances.

"I really would like to go back to Devon where we had our two holidays together with my mum and dad," said Eddie after a short pause.

"You mean Ludmouth."

"The very place."

"There won't be much to do there this time of the year, you know."

"I know but it would be fun anyway especially if old Mr Manders' ghost is still about in the shape of the local tramp."

"That always worried me, Eddie, you know."

"Why?"

"Because, if you remember, he grabbed us and pushed us out of the way of the train and saved our lives. How could a ghost do that, old son?"

"I don't know," said Eddie, "but I'm glad he did."

"Well, I don't think I can push people," said Len. "Let me try."

Len came right up to Eddie and put out his hands as if to push him.

"Can you feel anything?" asked Len.

"No, it just feels cold and odd."

"Odd?"

"Yes, it makes me want to take a step backwards but there was no physical sensation."

Len looked surprised.

"Maybe I can do it, then. With practice, I suppose I could probably push you backwards without you feeling anything. It's mind over matter, mate."

One or two people were beginning to pause and stare at Eddie as he was talking at the empty space in front of him. Some even asked him some obvious natural questions.

"Are you alright, son?"

"Did you say something?"

"Pardon – were you speaking to me?"

Ignoring the awkward queries, Eddie crossed over the road and headed down a narrow alleyway. Len followed, and when he had caught his friend up, they continued their conversation with Eddie leaning against a tall brick wall. He pretended to be looking through his wallet in case the occasional person passed by.

"So you want to go to Ludmouth, Eddie?"

"Do you remember much about it, Len?"

"Of course. Let me just concentrate and think."

Len wandered a few yards further down the alleyway with his ghostly head bowed to the ground. Eddie waited and expected a sudden and extreme change of light but, instead, Len's image got fainter and fainter until about twenty yards away it disappeared completely. Eddie followed cautiously until he reached the spot where his friendly ghost had vanished. Some invisible force seemed to prevent any further progress and, try as he might, he could not get any further down the alley. Even attempting to stay as close to either wall proved fruitless – there was no way through. A couple of young children walked towards him from the other side of the invisible barrier and giggled at his strange and frantic behaviour. Eddie began to concentrate his mind on Ludmouth and anything associated with the south Devon seaside resort – fossils, black sandy beach, their bed and breakfast and the rock tunnel. Nothing seemed to work. He needed the right code to pass through to the other side. Then it hit him – the code!

"Chocolate éclairs," he murmured and he tried immediately to walk through the invisible barrier. Suddenly, there was no longer any resistance and in flash of bright light, he passed through. Eddie was used to allowing his eyes adjust to the light and he kept them closed for a few seconds until, when he opened them again, he was astonished to find himself in almost total darkness. He reached out his hands to the front but felt nothing. He edged to his left until his shoulder touched something cold and hard – it was solid rock. He edged back to the right until again he felt solid rock. He was in a tunnel. It had to be the old abandoned railway tunnel that he and Len had explored when they had been on holiday in Ludmouth for the first time, now over two years ago. Eddie's voice echoed loudly even though he spoke quietly.

"Len? Where are you, Len?"

Apart from the faint noise of the sea from behind him, silence reigned in the tunnel. Len was not there. Eddie moved carefully forward until within a few yards he met the inner end of the tunnel, marked by an impenetrable pile of rocks and large boulders. Using one wall as a guide, he turned back and made for a possible outer exit to the tunnel in the direction from which the sound of the sea was coming. It had been blocked on the last occasion that he and Len had visited Ludmouth but it seemed to Eddie that it was his only possible means of escape. The darkness began to lighten as he approached the front of the tunnel. He could see daylight coming from a ragged hole at about head height in front of him. It looked small in diameter but Eddie knew he had to try it. One of his worst nightmares had always been crawling through underground tunnels only to find he reached a position where he could neither go forward or back, unable to move until the flesh dropped from his bones, by which time it would be too late! By moving a large rock into position to stand on, Eddie was able to haul his head and shoulders into the cavity; he hoped the rest of his torso would follow. His slimness, for once, was an advantage as he pulled himself through the hole. As his head emerged into bright sunlight, he started to recall all the derogatory name-calling he had received from fellow pupils during his life: '*Beanpole*', '*Skinny boy*' and, worst of all, '*Dipstick*'. By using both arms, he eased the rest of his body out onto the welcoming pile of rocks that rested against the cliff face. He slid and slithered in his prone position until he rolled onto the wet sand about five feet below. Apart from a few scrapes to his knees and elbows, he was unhurt. He turned over onto his back and breathed a huge sigh of relief. After a few moments, he raised himself into a sitting position and studied his surroundings. It was just as he remembered it – the red cliffs at Ludmouth on Devon's Jurassic Coast. It felt chilly and just like the sunny late autumn day that he'd left in Fenton-on-Sea, but was it Saturday, November the 27th 1965? His watch read ten forty-five.

Eddie brushed the wet sand and loose pieces of rock from his clothes and turned to walk the half mile to Ludmouth's Esplanade, the road that fronted the sandy beach and contained many of the better guest houses and small hotels. He felt in a more relaxed mood knowing that he had probably conquered one of the worst situations that he was likely to be faced with that day. Now all he had to do was find Len's ghost and, at least, he would have a passport back to the reality of Fenton-on-Sea.

Despite the uncomfortable realisation that he was totally alone in a place that was a day's journey from home, Eddie kept telling himself that Len was bound to put in an appearance sooner or later. Judging by how much it normally cost him to travel by train to Hamsden, he also thought that, if the worst came to the worst, he would have enough money to get a fair way home.

Ten minutes after emerging from the rock tunnel, he found himself standing opposite *Summer Breeze*, the guest house where his mum and dad had taken him and Len on two interesting summer holidays. He was still not totally convinced that he was in real time, but crossing over The Esplanade and peering through the window into the reception area, he could make out by the clock there that it was eleven o'clock exactly. Boldly, and without a thought for what he would say to the owner, affectionately known as BB, Eddie walked calmly inside.

Bob Brewin was standing behind the small counter in the reception area when Eddie made his entry. He didn't look up as Eddie approached and said,

"Surprise, BB!"

Bob Brewin still did not move or acknowledge Eddie's remark.

"It's me, BB – Eddie Compton. I've stayed with you a couple of times in the summer."

Still no response. Eddie began to raise his voice.

"I'm from Fenton-on-Sea. You must remember me."

While Eddie had been trying to communicate with BB, a guest had come down to reception. She was now standing uncomfortably close to Eddie and waiting to be attended to. BB looked up immediately and said,

"Good morning, Miss Taverner – going out?"

"Yes, BB, and I shan't be in for lunch."

"Well, have a good day. The weather looks set fair."

The elderly lady said goodbye and headed for the door. It began to dawn on Eddie – somehow between the tunnel and the guest house, he had become invisible! To double-check, he waved his arms frantically in front of BB's face but Bob Brewin eyes just followed Miss Taverner's exit from his guest house. He decided there was no point in remaining where he was and Eddie followed Miss Taverner out into the weak mid-morning sunshine. He recrossed The Esplanade and found a familiar seat on the promenade. He needed to think. Surely Len would come.

Eddie could see both the good side and bad side of his position. On the one hand, he could go unnoticed wherever he wanted, including boarding any relevant train that would get him home, but on the other, would he return to his normal physical state before he got there? The second question also raised another worrying problem in his mind. Had he been turned into a ghost and, if so, did that mean he was already …? Had something irreversible happened to him when he had followed Len through the invisible barrier in the alleyway back in Hamsden? If it had, did it also signify that Len's ghost had experienced a similar transformation which meant he had become invisible even to him? Without Len, he quickly realised that there was only going to be one solution to his problem. He had to make his way back to Hamsden by train and return to the alleyway. It was half past eleven by his watch and previous experience told him that it was at least a six hour journey, if all the connections were quick and smooth. Unfortunately, Ludmouth's nearest station was now at Ludmouth Junction and that was nearly three miles from where he sat. He calculated that he wouldn't get back to Hamsden until at least half past six that evening and so probably wouldn't make it home to Fenton until an hour later, given the probable detour to the invisible barrier. Shrugging his shoulders at the unavoidable decision, he got up from the seat to start the walk to the distant station. He crossed The Esplanade and quickly made his way up into the main town.

While he walked, Eddie thought about the excuse he could give his parents if he did actually arrive back late that evening. Normally, after the game on a Saturday, and even if he missed a train or dawdled, he would still be home no later than six-thirty. He had a couple of school friends that lived in Hamsden and he would say that he met one at the match and had gone home for tea with them. All that was necessary was a preliminary phone call which he would make from some convenient telephone box on his journey. Almost after he had sorted his plan, he realised that there was a huge problem with it. In addition to his invisibility, no one seemed to be able to hear him either. BB certainly hadn't heard him even when he had spoken loudly at the guest house. He broke into a trot as he entered the northern end of Ludmouth's residential area. He would just have to make every connection as quickly as he could. The 'tea-with-a-friend' excuse would have to suffice and without any prior warning to or permission from his parents.

Eddie found he couldn't make very quick progress along the disused track from the old Ludmouth station to the one still open at Ludmouth Junction. It had become overgrown and a dumping ground for rubbish of all kinds. Frightening memories of his and Len's narrow escape from the shunting engine came back to haunt him as he passed the spot of the near-tragic accident. It spurred him on to run and jump even more recklessly as he avoided broken sleepers and thick clumps of grass. He didn't reach the initial destination until nearly one o'clock and then discovered that the next train to Exeter wasn't until a quarter to two. He was fairly sure that direct trains ran to London at regular and frequent intervals from there. Some rough calculations from previous journeys home from Ludmouth suggested to Eddie that his original estimate of a six-thirty arrival at Hamsden would have to be revised. It was likely to be after eight o'clock with another hour or more needed to make it home finally. However, sitting on a platform seat in the bright and presumed November sunshine, hunger and thirst became his immediate concerns. He would have to procure something to eat and drink – it should be easy, given he was invisible. He dismissed any guilty thoughts about what he was going to do next as he headed for the small station buffet.

A meat pie and a bottle of cold milk satisfied Eddie's main physical needs. He left one traveller slightly bewildered when, having gone to the counter to get a knife and fork, he returned to discover his plate contained only vegetables. The milk had caused less consternation when it disappeared from a newly arrived crate on the platform. Without realising it, Eddie was fortunate that anything he touched, or indeed ate, became likewise invisible. He also managed to satisfy his curiosity as to the date when he spotted an overhead electric calendar which read:

November 27.

All connections were reasonably smooth and on time and Eddie found himself at London's Liverpool Street station at half past five. The various journeys had been interesting to say the least. Avoiding passengers sitting unknowingly on his lap was the worst difficulty and, in the end, he spent most of the way to London standing in the corridor. One young woman got a shock when she discovered a toilet was engaged only for the door to open mysteriously by itself as she waited for the non-existent person to vacate it! On several other occasions Eddie had to squeeze himself against the corridor side as people walked past him, sometimes discovering afterwards that part of their clothes had become disorganised or dislodged.

Eddie did, in the end, decide to make a phone call from a call box on platform seven; no one would notice the receiver raise itself upwards unaided. He would then argue later that he had tried to call his parents but he would tell them that he hadn't been able to make the connection. After his day wandering as a lost soul, it was cheering to hear the reality and comfort of his mum's voice when she answered his silent call.

"Hello, Fenton 3566."

"Hello? Who's speaking please?"

Eddie was also relieved to hear her third and final sentence.

"Hello, is that you, Eddie?"

After he had replaced the receiver, Eddie smiled, knowing that if he had been phoning from Hamsden on the way to a friend's house, he had chosen about the right time to make the call. His fictitious friend's parents, of course, were not on the phone.

The six o'clock train to Norwich and all intervening stations departed on time and Eddie reached Hamsden at twenty-five to eight. As soon as a young couple tried to walk straight through him as he walked along the platform, he knew that he had to head for the alleyway just off the town centre where he would try to restore himself to his natural visible form. It was a moonless night as Eddie threaded his way into town avoiding people off to the pubs or other places of entertainment on a Saturday evening. At first, he turned down the wrong alleyway and had to backtrack until he found the right one. For a few moments he was even panicked into thinking that the alleyway no longer existed and had disappeared along with Len's ghost. Reaching the spot where he had been transported to Devon that morning, he suddenly realised his mistake when the invisible barrier again stopped his progress. Despite his use of the special code, he could still not pass. He knew at once that he had to approach it from the other side. Peering through the gloom, illuminated only by a single weak neon street lamp, he tried to work out how he could get there. He retraced his steps to the first alleyway he'd tried and was relieved when it exited on a road parallel to the one at its entrance. He walked in the direction of where he thought that the correct alleyway ought also to exit but, to his horror, a six foot wooden fence blocked any possible way through. Eddie managed to find a knot hole to look through and, despite the gloom, could just make out that the real alleyway led into a builder's yard directly behind the fence. He looked round him – the quiet back street was deserted apart from a couple of squabbling cats. He reached up and grabbed the top of the fence with his bare hands. By using all his strength, he managed to haul himself into a position astride the fence and thence natural momentum and gravity provided the impetus for him to fall to the ground on the other side. He lay on his side for a few moments listening for noises but no one was about. Apart from a graze to one elbow which would not become visible until later, he was unhurt. He dusted himself down as best he could in the darkness and headed for the single street lamp which marked the alleyway he needed.

"Chocolate éclairs," he whispered as he stood where he thought the barrier to be. Suddenly, as before, the darkness was lifted in a bright flash of white light and Eddie walked casually through.

"*Just in time for the game, Captain.*"

Eddie rubbed his eyes and looked at his watch. It was a quarter past two. Len stood grinning in the alleyway.

"Well done, Eddie. I knew you had the resources to accomplish the little mission I set you."

"Little? It was a nightmare at times, Len. I thought you were coming with me."

"I never said I was, you know. I just asked how you would get back without me. It appears that you still have some of your old powers."

"I didn't do anything special."

"But it helped that you were invisible, eh?"

"You knew that would happen?"

I guessed it might when I set up my plan for you. After all if you can see me when I'm a ghost why can't you develop other powers too? I somehow knew it had happened when you came through the barrier."

"Where did you go to?"

"Nowhere – I sensed you had reached the rock tunnel and then I went into one of my suspended periods. The next thing I knew was when you said the special code for the second time and I returned here. I have no knowledge of what you did after you reached Ludmouth. You'll have to tell me sometime. Now go and enjoy the rest of your day. All this scheming and thinking has exhausted me. I'll be in touch very soon. You're turning into a trainee ghost, Captain."

Len vanished before Eddie had a chance to reply. It had been an extraordinary day so far. It took on a stranger twist when Eddie looked down at his dusty duffle coat and the slight tear in the right elbow.

19

I Could Have Been Anything

As far as it was possible for Eddie, he enjoyed the rest of his extended day out. Town gained a creditable 1-1 draw against a side ten places above them in the league, but when he arrived home at five to six that evening, his mother was the first to spoil his euphoria.

"What on earth have you been doing, Eddie? Your coat is in such a mess."

"It's nothing, Mum. I was pushed to the ground at the game and grazed my elbow, I think."

Eddie's dad entered the questioning.

"Did you get me my programme?"

"Oh sorry, Dad, I forgot. You can have mine – I don't need it."

Eddie was made to go and have a hot bath before his tea and, afterwards, his mother applied loving care and a plaster to his elbow. He went to bed very early that night having been out of the house for nearly fifteen hours, whether real or imagined. He slept fairly well, despite his mind trying to get to grips with the new twist in his relationship with ghosts. Ought he to be worried that he had become one for a few hours?

The weeks up to Christmas seemed to pass slowly for Eddie and he wasn't sure that he was content with his ordinary life as it became in those days. No more nightmares, strange events or visits from ghosts, whether Len's or not, impinged on his waking or sleeping moments. The school term finished on Friday, December the 17th and thoughts turned to Christmas shopping. The previous two Saturdays since the 'trip' to Devon had been spent for Eddie mostly inside owing to the inclement weather. When he awoke on the morning following the end of term, blue sky coupled with a crisp and cold atmosphere led him to recalling that extraordinary day. Though much colder, the day had a similar feel to it and at breakfast he announced to his mother,

"Town are home today, so I think I'll spend the morning in Hamsden doing some Christmas shopping and then go to the game."

"Well, if you do, don't go and get into any trouble like last time. I don't want to have to repair your coat again."

Eddie mumbled something about it having not been his fault but knew he couldn't guarantee that some kind of 'trouble' might not come his way if Len put in an appearance.

Eddie was not as anxious to leave so early as the last time – he didn't want another unnaturally long day if his friend should have plans for him. He caught the ten-forty train from the station and was in Hamsden at ten past the hour. The journey had been an uncomfortable one with the train packed with Christmas shoppers and a few early football fans. Eddie stood all the way watching continually for any ghostly appearances. There were none and he was somewhat relieved when he was able to stretch his legs down Station Road on his way into town. He had one initial destination in mind.

The alleyway looked the same as it had done before, infrequently used except by the residents of the few houses on each side. The vehicle entry to the builder's yard was located in a neighbouring street that bordered it. Pedestrians only used the alleyway on weekdays to gain entry to the yard. Eddie approached the invisible line with caution, both hands out in front of him feeling for the obstruction. He felt nothing as he passed the street lamp that had marked the barrier previously. He walked to the end of the alleyway and retraced his steps several times but without anything impeding his progress. He'd already decided in his mind the next destination if the alleyway proved fruitless in his search for Len and the excitement he might bring.

Osborne's was as busy as anyone could ever remember and the toy section was probably the busiest of all the departments. Eddie was jostled and pushed in all directions until an alcove in a wall provided a safe haven for a few minutes where he could also observe his surroundings. He didn't have to wait long until his friend put in an appearance. A tall burly security guard was making his rounds in the toy department and quickly spotted Eddie apparently loitering in the quiet corner he had found.

"Now then, Captain, we can't have you just hanging around here – not unless you're going to buy something. How have you been, Eddie?"

The speaker was a tall, fair-haired man in his middle to late thirties and, though handsome, he had clearly seen better days. Some tattoos on his wrists and hands indicated that he had been a boxer at some time in the past and he had the air of someone who had been used to mixing with the more criminal element of society. Eddie could see a silver chain around his neck, though not what hung at its lowest point which was hidden underneath a smart shirt and tie. He continued to speak when Eddie seemed reluctant to reply to his original question.

"Don't be scared. I can be anything I want now, Eddie, just like you were able to go anywhere you wanted to last time, so I can choose to be all the people I never got a chance to be. I always fancied a security guard's job – plenty of perks, eh? Easier than being a footballer as well."

Edie began to relax. This was another new twist – his friend could now change form at will. 'Len' ushered Eddie away from his safe haven and said,

"Come on, you'll have to move from there. I'll get the sack if I don't move you on. I'll see you in about half an hour when I take my break for a smoke. I'll be waiting for you out the back at the goods entrance. I may be in another form. I always fancied being a policeman!"

Eddie nodded as 'Len' moved to let him pass. He continued to say nothing as he made his way quickly through the crowds and out of the toy department. Once out of the shop, he had a chance to ponder the brief meeting. Had it been the real Len? How otherwise could he have known about the trip to Devon? Eddie cursed his stupidity for not asking for the code word. He would have to satisfy his curiosity in a few minutes time, but he was beginning to guess what conclusion he would reach – Len had hated people who smoked and boxing had always been about his least favourite sport.

Eddie waited at the back entrance to Osborne's for at least twenty minutes past the supposed time for 'Len's' break. It soon occurred to him that the evil ghost had only ever appeared in Osborne's toy department, thus almost confirming his growing suspicions. He was also not that surprised when, after another few minutes, a young policeman approached him to ask him why he was hanging around in such an unusual place.

"Come along me lad. Move along. Move along."

Even the policeman's language seemed contrived and stereotyped and when Eddie stood his ground and grinned cheekily, it got worse.

"On your way, sunshine or I'll book you for loitering with intent. Move along now."

Eddie at last made his coded reply.

"I'll go, officer, if you give me a chocolate éclair."

The policeman was clearly not amused.

"Right that's enough cheek from you, my lad. You are coming with me to the station."

Although his suspicions were now totally confirmed, Eddie realised also that he had pushed his luck almost too far as the policeman made a grab for him. Another voice shouted from over his shoulder.

"*Run, Eddie. Run as fast as you can, mate.*"

Eddie turned and ran as the voice had commanded him. He felt a cold and clammy grip on his left wrist but his momentum quickly broke it and within seconds he was out of sight of the evil ghost. Pausing for breath at the junction with the High Street, he was relieved to see Len's good ghost standing waiting for him. Eddie positioned himself so that no one passing would see him speaking. Len then said,

"Well done, my boy. That was a close one."

"You're not kidding. I should have checked straightaway with the code word."

"We may have to use a different one from now on, now that he's heard it," said Len. "Have you got any ideas for something that I wouldn't already know and is particularly unusual?"

Eddie thought for a moment and then said,

"My mum's middle name."

"Which is?"

"Blythe"

"That *is* unusual. Let's just hope that my evil ghost isn't listening."

"He didn't seem to recognise the first code. He was too busy showing off as a policeman."

Len seemed satisfied but he was also curious as to how Eddie's suspicions had first been raised.

"What initially made you think the ghost wasn't me?"

"Because he smoked and had obviously been a boxer and when he said he always wanted to be a policeman, I knew for sure."

"How so?"

"Well, you would never smoke; you hated boxing and policeman even more! They would be the kind of things that …."

Len interrupted to finish Eddie's sentence.

"Only my evil side would like, eh?"

"Yes, precisely, and that's how I knew he was evil."

Len smiled at his friend's astute reading of the situation but had a warning for his living friend.

"Just be careful if he plays a double bluff and appears to you in one of my favourite occupations, like a footballer."

Eddie raised his eyebrows in agreement. He had had a lucky escape but he had to ask Len one more question concerning it.

"How did he know I'd been somewhere I wanted to last time we met, Len?"

"Simple, mate. I still have a small part of me that is evil and devious and that part was able to convey the information to my evil ghost. I've told you before that we are all made up of good and bad. The ghost you saw was how I could have become if I'd lived and allowed my evil side to dominate. Some people, like murderers and rapists, let their evil sides take over completely and even rid themselves of any vestige of conscience that they might have left."

Eddie liked it when Len made it seem so simple and he smiled inwardly at the irony that in death, Len appeared to be the more intelligent and thoughtful person. By the time Eddie had absorbed all that the good ghost had said, Len's image had already begun to fade and just before it vanished completely, he heard Len say,

"Have a good day, Eddie. I may see you later, and this time, use the new code immediately."

Eddie could hardly believe the time by his watch after Len had left him. It was already past two o'clock. Whereas two weeks earlier, he had gained several hours, this time he was convinced that he had lost about an hour. He quickly grabbed a sandwich and a drink from Pritchard's Coffee House and headed for Freeman Street. It looked like there was going to be a large crowd at the game; many husbands and their sons had had enough of Christmas shopping for one day.

Local rivals, Borchester United were to be Town's opponents and they had brought a large contingent of fans from the small market town thirty miles to the north of Hamsden. As soon as Eddie had got into the North Stand, it was clear to him that there was going to be a capacity gate of over 12,000. Try as he might, he found he was far too late to get a position behind the goal and eventually he ended up no more than a few feet from where he had come into the stand. During the game he adopted a relaxed posture that allowed him to sway with the crowd around him; it being impossible to resist the movement, at times, which mirrored an undulating wave of the sea.

Hamsden Town won the game 2–1 with both the home goals being scored by Eddie's favourite centre forward, Johnny McBride. Getting out of the ground proved a struggle for Eddie's slimly built frame and by the time he had reached Station Road he was exhausted. After the sunny December day, a thick damp fog had begun to descend on the crocodile of fans that made its way up to the station. By the time Eddie had reached it, his coat and ginger hair were wet with drops of water. Many more fans seemed to have opted for the trains in preference to the buses – rumours had already started that some had been cancelled due to the denseness of the fog. Eddie found he was too late to catch the first train back to Fenton; it was packed almost beyond safety. Since the next one was not until ten to six, he decided to get a cup of tea in the station café. It was surprisingly empty and he was able to sit by himself at an isolated table near the door. The sound of laughter could be heard from the bar next to the café where many fans had repaired for a post-match drink. The warmth of the café had a soporific effect on Eddie and despite his cup of tea, he struggled to keep his eyes open.

"Is this chair taken?"

Eddie tried to focus his heavy-lidded eyes on the owner of the voice. It belonged to a tall elderly man with distinguished silky grey hair.

"N-no, sir," stammered Eddie in a whispered voice.

"Thank you, young man. Have you been to the game, Captain?"

The old man sat down and Eddie smiled.

"Len?"

"Of course, Eddie."

Eddie looked thoughtful.

'*This has to be the good ghost. He's such a friendly and nice looking man, but ....*'

"Such a Blythe game," he said.

"Would that be spelt with a 'y' like your mum's middle name, Eddie?"

"It really is you Len!"

"Yes, and well done. I thought you'd failed the test."

Now he had been shaken wide awake, Eddie found he could recognise his friend's voice, although it came from the mouth of a man who appeared to be well into his sixties.

"Who are you supposed to be, Len?"

"How about a retired doctor?"

Eddie was silent while some people made their way out of the café. One lingered by the door as if he had forgotten something. Eddie frowned

– had he heard him talking to the empty chair in front of him? When the man had gone, Eddie asked,

"Is that what you always wanted to be, then – a doctor?"

"I've always admired them for what they do, but I never wanted to be one. I just wasn't clever enough. Now I can pretend. Isn't it fun?"

Eddie was not so sure.

"It's not that good when people can't see you."

"You can, mate, and that's important to me. Could I pass for a retired doctor?"

"Yes, I suppose so. Do you feel like one?"

"Stupid question, Eddie. I've told you before that I don't feel things. I just imagined what I thought a retired doctor would look like and here I am. Another good trick, eh?"

"It's your good side doing it, then?"

"Yes. Good attracts good, I suppose, like my evil ghost associated himself with bad people."

"The police aren't bad."

"I think the one who tried to grab you was, mate. He had all the hallmarks of a bent copper."

Eddie nodded. Len looked tired and he added,

"You'll have to catch you train soon. I just wanted you to know that we ghosts can appear in many different forms. I could have been anything, you know. Evil should not be allowed to have all the fun."

In the time it took Eddie to look out the door to see the next Fenton train arriving, Len had disappeared.

In the train on the way home that foggy December night, Eddie amused himself by considering the idea of Len as a doctor in real life: issuing wrong prescriptions; recommending the wrong leg for amputation;

diagnosing an incurable disease instead of flu – the list was endless. 'Stick to being a footballer, Len', he thought.

20

A Shady Deal from the Past

Ann Blythe Compton seemed more cheerful than Eddie expected when he got home just after twenty to seven; the train's progress had been slow owing to the dense fog but, surprisingly, his mother didn't seem as though she had been unduly worried. She met him the hall and handed him a towel to dry his wet face and hair.

"Sorry I'm late, Mum. I couldn't get on the first train and then we travelled at less than thirty all the way home."

"That's alright, dear. I expected as much," she replied with a smile. "I have some news, Eddie."

"What, Mum?"

"Aunty Martha's coming for Christmas."

"What? On her own?"

"Yes, love. What a silly question."

Eddie realised that he'd almost said too much with regards to Martha Wilby's possible new companion. That was for the future.

"Good show," said Eddie as quickly as he could. "When she's coming?"

"Christmas Eve. Your dad'll pick her up from the station."

Later, in his room, Eddie decided it would be nice to have Len's mum to stay. Apart from the certainty of a Christmas present from her, it would also provide a link to his best friend. It would be interesting to hear his auntie's news since she had lost her husband and son. Had she received ghostly visits from Len that she'd been aware of? Maybe, also, Len would use the opportunity to put in an appearance.

Eddie's dad duly picked Martha Wilby up from the station at five-thirty on the afternoon of Christmas Eve – he had finished work at four and had been able to get home to fetch his car for the purpose. She looked attractively dressed as she walked down platform one to meet Fred. After a quick peck on the cheek, Eddie's dad carried her small suitcase to the waiting Hillman Minx. Fred had expected his wife's best friend to look sad and dowdy but the woman who sat beside him in his new car was far from that. Her hair had been permed in an ultra-modern style and her pale green suit looked like one of the latest London fashions. Extra make-up and red lipstick combined to make her look ten years younger. She was clearly at one with the world and enjoying life. Eddie's dad swung the Hillman off the station forecourt and into the High Street.

"New car, Fred?" asked Martha.

"Not brand new, Martha. The Morris Minor had just about had it, I'm afraid."

"I'm going to get a car," said Martha. "I'm learning to drive."

"Good," said Fred as they turned into South Road. "It'll get you out and about again after ...."

"Don't be afraid to say it, Fred. You mean after Cyril and Len died. Life has to go on you know."

As he pulled the car onto the drive of number 38 Fir Tree Close, Fred Compton wondered if all the make-up and new clothes were a normal part of Martha's daily image and, if so, was there someone special that they were for?

The two women hugged each other for an almost abnormally long time with Eddie's mum in tears and barely able to speak. Her friend seemed to be much more in control of the emotional situation.

"Now, now, Ann. Please don't cry. It's so good to see you and Fred."

Martha gently pushed Ann into a position where she could look into her wet eyes.

"I'm alright, Ann, you know. Really I am. Now where's Eddie?"

Eddie emerged from behind his mum and gave his 'aunty' a hug. She smelt of exotic perfume; quite unlike his best friend's mum that he'd known when Len had been alive.

"You've grown taller, Eddie and filled out a little. You're making a nice young man."

Martha paused and for the first time since arriving, she looked sad.

"Len would have been fifteen just over a week ago, you know."

Eddie wondered how his aunty would have reacted if he had told her that he had recently seen her son in the café on Hamsden station and that he had looked at least twenty years older than her!

Christmas Day arrived with a significant change in the weather. As if by celestial command, the day dawned free of fog with a deep golden sun in a clear blue sky. Eddie awoke in the somewhat pleasurable knowledge that it would be the first Christmas that his sister would not be at home. She was spending the long weekend with her boyfriend's parents, Mr and Mrs Jones. She would go straight from there to do some holiday work at Arleson's the bakers on the Tuesday. She needed whatever money she could get while she was at college.

When presents were exchanged under the tree, Eddie appeared to be a little nervous as he started to open his from Len's mum. Surely it couldn't be Len's railway timetable, could it? He was relieved when he discovered a book on mathematical tricks and puzzles together with a five-pound note tucked inside – more money than he had received from all his other real aunties and uncles combined. He was understandably ecstatic.

"Wow! Thanks, Aunty Martha."

"That's alright, Eddie. I don't have Len to buy for this year."

Eddie replied in like vein.

"Neither do I. I got him a card though – it's upstairs. You can have it if you like."

"That would be nice, Eddie. Thank you."

Eddie thoroughly enjoyed the main two days of Christmas with Len's mum and his own parents. With the Monday a public holiday as well, the normal festivities were extended into a third day. It was clear from a chat that he had on the evening of the 27th that Len's mum had not had any supernatural encounters with her dead son. She and Eddie had been delegated to do the washing-up after another enormous meal while Eddie's parents took a well-earned rest in the lounge. Eddie was bold enough to start what he knew might be a difficult conversation.

"Do you talk to Len, Aunty Martha?"

Martha Wilby looked a little oddly at Eddie.

"No, dear, I don't – at least not for some time. We have to move on and not dwell in the past. I know he's gone to a much better place and talking to empty space would only be self-indulgent, you know."

'If only you knew', thought Eddie as Len's mum continued.

"I used to talk to both of them and I'd get so annoyed with Len's dad in particular, for driving so fast that day, but I soon decided that it was pointless apportioning blame. He didn't do it on purpose and what's done is done."

"You do believe in God though, don't you?" asked Eddie.

"Yes, I suppose so – most of the time anyway. What about you, Eddie?"

"Oh yes, I believe in God."

"Do you also believe that you'll see Len again one day?"

Eddie knew he would never be able to say what he ought to say and managed instead,

"Maybe, but not in the same form as he was when he was alive."

If Len had been watching, Eddie hoped he would be 'patting him on the back' with a ghostly hand. After Martha gave Eddie a comforting hug, the conversation moved on to less ethereal and less difficult topics and the washing-up concluded in harmony.

Martha Wilby returned to Petersgate by train on the morning of Tuesday the 28th with some sadness for Eddie. He had warmed to Len's mum's new approach to life over her short stay. In addition, he was disappointed that her son had not deigned to put in an appearance over the festive period. Surely he could have made the effort.

The sales had already begun in earnest when Eddie wandered into town the following day. The unusually sunny and dry weather was continuing as he headed for Fenton-on-Sea's limited range of shops with money to spend. As he entered the High Street, he had an uncomfortable felling of déjà vu. As if on cue, a familiar voice called from behind him as he passed the station forecourt and it immediately brought back memories of a Saturday morning almost exactly to the day three years previously.

"*What ho, sport!*"

Eddie stopped to usher Len's ghost behind the high station wall, where he could speak out of sight and earshot. This time, he knew he had to confirm the speaker's identity before he started any conversation.

"Whatcha blithe comrade."

"Is that with a 'Y' or an 'I'?"

"You tell me," replied Eddie now facing the ghost full on.

"Depends how your mum spells it, mate."

"It's you at last, Len. Where have you been?"

"Nowhere, mate. The last thing I remember was pretending to be a retired and respected doctor of medicine who was taking time out of his busy schedule to talk to you on a foggy December night on Hamsden station. Christmas has obviously come and gone."

"Yes and we've had your mum to stay for a few days. She went home yesterday."

"How ironic that I should miss her when she came back to Fenton-on-Sea. How did she seem?"

"She's well, Len, and seems to be getting on with life – new clothes and hair-do. She looked happy."

"Did she mention me and Dad?"

"Only briefly, mate. She doesn't blame your dad for the accident and she still loves you. She bought me a Maths book and gave me five pounds for Christmas."

"Lucky sod. She never spent that much on me when I was alive."

Eddie's position was becoming exposed as more people started to filter into the forecourt for the trains to Hamsden. Len followed the high wall until he found a large oak tree which would hide his friend from view completely. Eddie stood with his back to the wall as if studying the trunk of the old tree.

"You know what my dad thinks, Len?"

"What?"

"He told me he thinks she might have a new man in her life."

Len smiled and Eddie thought he seemed pleased, but he decided against telling him about Michael Conners, the teacher who had been at the funeral. He didn't think that Len needed to know just yet about the future long-lasting relationship between Mr Conners and his mum which had probably had its inception at his and his dad's wake! Eddie changed the subject.

"Why have you come today?" he asked with some excitement in his voice.

"Just to try something out, Eddie."

"What?"

"You'll see – just follow me."

Eddie watched as Len's good ghost began walking quickly for the station exit. He seemed to glide over the ground and was almost lost to Eddie's sight before he knew it. He had to run quickly in order to catch him up fifty yards or so down the High Street. The town was too busy for words to be exchanged without causing curiosity and Len held a finger to his lips when Eddie was about to say something. Five minutes later and Len had led his friend to the turning into Mill Road. It suddenly dawned on Eddie where Len was going. It had become cloudy overhead and by the time he had reached Watson's Electrical it was strangely dark. Within seconds the light had vanished completely and Eddie struggled to find the shopfront. Something was happening again and he just hoped his friendly ghost was in sole charge. After a few seconds, the darkness started to lift gradually. Eddie immediately felt different, somehow smaller and not quite himself and when he caught sight of his own reflection in the shop window, all was revealed. He looked to be about twelve and was wearing clothes that he hadn't seen for several years. Len was nowhere to be seen. A voice came from the shop doorway.

"Well, are you coming in or not, Eddie?"

Len had already entered the shop and had poked his head out to see where his friend had got to. He looked much younger too and when Eddie raised his eyes to read the sign over the shop, he knew finally what had happened. In place of what should have been a sign advertising Watson's Electrical, Eddie read,

'*Canter's Junk Shop*'.

Eddie knew what it signified. He had gone back in time to a similar day just after Christmas in 1962 when he and Len had once before gone into the junk shop with money to spend. Before he followed Len's ghost into the shop, memories of several fantastic adventures flashed through his mind. He had the mind of a fourteen-year-old but it was trapped inside an eleven-year-old body. This was going to be interesting to say the least!

Len was standing in a corner away from the shop counter when Eddie entered. He could see from the expression on his face that he also was aware of what had happened. Eddie turned back to the counter to face the smiling and apparently friendly face of Mr George Counter. He too looked exactly as he had done on that Saturday three years ago.

"Well what do you want, my boy?"

Even the words seemed to be familiar to Eddie and when he replied he didn't seem to be in control of the situation.

"I just wondered if you had any science fiction books in, Mr Canter, sir."

'This was not right', thought Eddie. 'Why had he been so formal?' Len was still watching from the corner of the shop. George didn't seem to have noticed him.

"Of course I have. Just let me fetch them – you can have them for next to nothing, Eddie."

After George had disappeared into the back of his shop, Len came over to Eddie and whispered in his ear.

"Be careful, Eddie. Be very careful. Watch out for his tricks."

Eddie knew what 'tricks' Len was referring to and he nodded in silence.

Almost immediately, George emerged from his back rooms carrying a pile of magazines which he placed ceremoniously on the counter.

"Here you are, Eddie my boy. There must be twenty or more."

Again Eddie found himself replying as though from memory. He was not in control of his thoughts or his voice.

"What do you want for them, sir?"

"Well to you, Eddie, I charge one shilling only."

Eddie was beginning to see where the deal was going but, once again, he played his part unwittingly.

"I'll take them please, Mr Canter."

Eddie produced his wallet from his pocket and extracted the crisp new five-pound note that his aunty Martha had given him. He handed it swiftly to George Canter and, without waiting for any change, took the pile of magazines from the counter and turned to make his way out of the shop. As he did so, George turned back to his till, opened it and was just about to deposit the note there when Eddie caught a glimpse of Len moving quickly towards the counter. He thought he heard his friendly ghost shout,

"Run, Eddie! Run!"

In a flash and with seemingly impossibly long arms, Len reached over and grabbed the note from George's hands. George, for his part, looked both shocked and relieved – almost as if he knew what he had been about to do was wrong. By this time, Eddie had dropped the pile of magazines and was running out of the shop. If he had glanced back, he would have seen the sight of George Canter scrabbling frantically on the floor behind the counter but, of course, he wouldn't find the note that he thought had been blown out of his hand by a sudden draught.

The weather and light had returned to normal when Eddie reached the pavement outside the shop. Len was waiting for him across the other side of Mill Road where he was watching some customers enter the shop Eddie had just vacated. Once again, the sign above it advertised Watson's Electrical. Eddie crossed over to meet his friend. Len smiled and pointed to the pavement beside his foot and Eddie immediately bent down to pick up his five-pound note.

"That was a close one, Captain," said Len.

Eddie positioned himself with his back to a lamp post and pretended to be looking in a shop window. Len came and stood beside him.

"Too close for comfort, Len," replied Eddie. "What was that all about? Why did you let that happen?"

"I arranged my little demonstration just to show you that everyone has an evil side, including our sadly departed friend George."

"So that was his evil ghost?"

"Got it in one, mate. That's how he used to be before he went back to Poland. Of course, he did repay everyone he'd robbed by his former shady dealings and even though he didn't know why he was doing it, he was aware that it was wrong."

"So he has two ghosts; one evil and one good?"

"Everyone has, Eddie, I think."

A couple of people had, by this time, joined Eddie in browsing in *Needles and Pins*, Fenton's dress-making shop. Eddie began to walk back up Mill Road to the High Street. Len went on ahead and began to show off to Eddie by dodging the cars and bicycles in the road. Five minutes later, and with Eddie out of breath from his run through town, Len had led him to the deserted beach at the bottom of Steep Hill. Eddie followed his friendly ghost right to the water's edge. Facing the sea and in a breathless voice, Eddie said,

"What's the hurry, Len?"

"No hurry, Captain – just trying to keep you fit."

After a pause, he continued.

"Now you are beginning to understand the difference between good and evil, I hope. Evil must never be allowed to triumph but it is always there even …."

"Even?"

"Even after death, Eddie. You already know that I can still be bad – you've met my evil ghost and, you never know, there maybe more than one of them."

Eddie thought about it for a moment, but in the end decided against asking Len if there could be more than one of his good ghosts as well. It could prove the start of a long and difficult discussion and Len looked tired again. The morning's demonstration seemed to have taken a lot out of him.

"I'm going now, Eddie. Look after yourself and be careful when you talk to ghosts. Even close and respected friends can be bad."

After he had spoken these last words, Len seemed to walk a few paces into the shallow water. Without a splash or even a ripple of any kind, he vanished into the sea.

21

Evil Returns

Eddie didn't remain down town for very much longer after his encounter with Mr Canter's evil ghost. He too was at least mentally tired and, unless he made the trip to Hamsden, Fenton-on-Sea's shops really didn't have much to offer a fourteen-year-old boy, especially one of Eddie's intelligence. Indeed, the excitement and wonder of the previous few months had begun to make any normal earthly pursuits seem trivial at best. Life was good, yes, but death seemed to provide more interesting and unusual avenues.

Eddie did make a trip to Hamsden but not until 1966 had started. He was due back at school for the spring term on Wednesday, January the 5th and he decided to take the train early on the Tuesday morning. He had found the previous six days a little mundane and had spent them mostly working through his new mathematical puzzle book and some forgotten school work. Town were not at home; they had a third round F.A. Cup tie against a side a division above them so Eddie hoped the crowds would not be too large despite the New Year sales still being in full swing. He caught the ten past nine train as usual with every intention of being back well before lunchtime. He was in a good mood when he reached Hamsden after no alarms or ghostly visitations and having been able to sit all the way. The weather, though damp, was unseasonably mild and Eddie felt a little warm in his school duffle coat.

Before he got to the town centre proper, Eddie had already made a tentative decision not to visit Osborne's, concentrating, instead, on the few but well-stocked bookshops. He met Sally Barber from school for a brief chat outside Pritchard's Coffee House but, despite some perceived gentle encouragement, he didn't invite her to go inside with the standard,

'Fancy a coffee?' routine. After five minutes, they parted without Eddie really realising that the young lady in question had more than a soft spot for her intelligent fellow fourth year.

By eleven o'clock, Eddie had exhausted all the possibilities of things to do or buy in Hamsden and with some inevitability about the decision he made his way towards Osborne's department store. One small paperback on famous Mathematicians in British history was his sole purchase of the morning. Within ten minutes he had reached the toy department on the top floor. It was far less busy than the Saturday before Christmas when he had had the confrontation with the security guard but no such person seemed to be around this time. 'Action Man' was the latest craze on sale in Osborne's and though more entertaining than the normal run-of-the-mill toys, it didn't appeal to Eddie's inquiring mind despite its fantasy overtones. An eager sales assistant approached him and the young man asked politely,

"Is there anything I can help you with?"

"No thanks, I'm just looking," replied Eddie with equal politeness.

The young assistant smiled while Eddie studied his features carefully. With some disappointment, he quickly decided that, however good a disguise the assistant might be sporting, he definitely wasn't Len. The young man moved on to speak to someone else.

"*You're beginning to see me everywhere, Captain.*"

At first, Eddie thought the voice was coming from entirely within his own head but a quick glance to his left revealed Len grinning from ear to ear. Because he had been taken off guard, Eddie had forgotten the essential identification routine and replied,

"I knew you would come, mate."

Len shook his head with resignation and said,

"Haven't you forgotten something?"

Eddie realised his mistake and without trying to make any sense, said,

"Sorry, you caught me at a blithe moment."

"Is that spelt with an 'I' or a 'Y'?"

"Same way as the woman's name."

Len paused and then said,

"So that's with a 'Y', then, like your mum?"

"Yes, comrade Len. It's good to see you."

"*Who are you talking to, Eddie?*"

This time, the second familiar voice came from his right and Eddie turned sharply round. A second and identically dressed Len stood less than six feet away. The new ghost continued.

"I told you last time to be very careful when you spoke to anyone, Captain. I presume you're talking to one of my ghosts."

"Yes, and the real one as well," replied Eddie sarcastically.

"The real one? How do you know he's the real one?"

"Because he knew the code."

"And what is the code, then, Eddie?"

Eddie grinned at the pathetic attempt to draw the special signal out of him. This bad ghost wasn't very clever!

"Nice try," he said.

"Well, let me see now. I wonder if it could be your mother's middle name."

Eddie's grin receded slightly. He couldn't possibly know, could he?

The 'good' ghost entered the conversation from Eddie's left.

"He doesn't know, Eddie. Ask him what it is."

He called the evil ghost's bluff.

"Which is?"

"How about Blythe?"

"Is that with an 'I' or a 'Y'?"

"A 'Y' of course."

Though they clearly couldn't see each other, the new ghost moved past Eddie and stood unknowingly side by side with the first one. Eddie could now see them both together for the first time and he realised that he had a problem. Little did he know, but in a moment it would get worse. In the meantime, he studied each ghost carefully. He had been totally convinced that the first had been the real one but now he was not so sure. They had both sounded like Len's good ghost and they were identical in every other respect. They had both passed the security check with ease too. The second ghost had a slight advantage in that he knew he had warned Eddie to be careful on a previous occasion but that proved nothing really. Both ghosts came from the same person anyway. Matters then took an awkward twist. As if they were being orchestrated by another power, both ghosts swapped position and then, to Eddie's horror, they did it again and again, until after a dozen or more swaps, he was totally confused as to which ghost was which. His eyes had become fogged in the process of trying to keep track of either or both of them in their macabre dance. To make matters worse, the young shop assistant returned and said to Eddie,

"Are you alright, young man? You look like you've seen a ghost."

Eddie mumbled that he was fine and waited where he was until the assistant was out of sight. Eddie knew that the sensible thing to do was to get out of the store as quickly as possible particularly if both ghosts were evil ones! Curiosity, however, got the better of him.

"*You've got to choose one of us,*" said one ghost.

"*You've got to choose one of us,*" said the other.

Whether this was mimicry or not, Eddie wasn't sure. If they couldn't see each other they probably couldn't hear each other either, he thought. Two voices then echoed in his head:

"Choose good or evil."

"Choose evil or good."

"Good or evil."

"Evil or good."

"Good or evil."

"Evil or ...."

The voices were incessant. Some shoppers stopped to look at Eddie who was now transfixed and staring into space. He had to choose and quickly too. He couldn't understand why but it felt like his life depended on it – almost as if he made the wrong choice he would be damned forever. The odds were even. It was the worst possible choice to have to make even though millions of gamblers did it everyday but only for money. This seemed to Eddie to be a matter of life or death. He closed his eyes and prayed.

'O God, help me choose right. I want to choose good, not evil.'

Eddie opened his eyes. He didn't have to make the choice. Only one ghost remained in front of him. After a few seconds, Eddie regained his composure. He had faced his most frightening choice ever and had survived. Len indicated to Eddie to follow him and a few minutes later they were both in a quiet side street just off the town centre. Len was first to break the tension.

"Good always triumphs over evil."

Len could tell that Eddie was still nervous when he said,

"How do I know that you *are* the good ghost, Len?"

"You don't, I suppose. It's a matter of faith. Do you want me to be the real ghost?"

"That would be a difficult question if you're not."

"Have faith, Eddie. I am the good ghost. Take a look behind you."

Eddie turned to look back up the street to the shops. He could just make out the other ghost, smoking a cigarette and clearly up to no good. He appeared to be arguing with a young woman and had hold of her handbag which he was trying to steal. Moments later and two men had freed the bag from his grip but then they themselves suffered abuse, both verbal and physical, as Len's evil ghost threw wild punches in all directions. Eddie was convinced and he turned back to Len to apologise for doubting him. The good ghost had vanished.

22
Snow

After Len's abrupt disappearance, Eddie returned home quickly that morning without further alarm or hindrance. It had been an interesting excursion to say the least though he was not altogether sure that he should read too much into it. It had been a lively demonstration of the battle between good and evil, it was true, but as to it having any significance for his future he had his doubts. Indeed, his immediate future was definitely concerned with harsh reality and the return to school the following day. Len was lucky in the fact that he could continually amuse himself and others with the fight against the darker forces at work within the human psyche and in the universe at large. Eddie definitely did not have the time or inclination to continue to dwell on such issues – final preparations were needed ahead of the spring term.

Eddie had not spoken to his sister for some time about George Canter's warning to her so it was with some surprise that she came to see him in his room just before he was going to bed. She stood nervously in the doorway until Eddie invited her to come in.

"What's up, sister dear?"

"I just wanted to wish you luck for the new term, Eddie."

Eddie looked up in disbelief. It was not the kind of thing that Jenny would even think about let alone say! There had to be a reason.

"Why? Do you know something I don't?"

"No, I just remembered what that man or ghost said to me about you having to be careful."

"What, Mr Canter?"

"Yes, him."

"Have you seen him again, then?"

"No, not really."

"Come on, Jenny. You either have or you haven't. Which is it?"

"I had a dream last night and in it he came to the door as before and said more or less the same thing to me again."

"Dreams are just dreams, Jenny," said Eddie.

"I know and I don't usually remember them but this one I did."

"What else do you remember?" asked Eddie trying not to show too much interest.

"Not much more than that which happened for real back in November. This time I ran after him straightaway but he was always just out of reach. He went out of our road again and followed South Road into the High Street and down Mill Road where he seemed to disappear into what must have been his old shop. I seemed to follow him in and ...."

"And?"

"And there was nothing there – nothing but a big black hole and I couldn't stop myself from falling and falling until I woke up in a cold sweat. When I woke up this morning I didn't really remember much about the dream and it's only been this evening that I've managed to piece it altogether."

Eddie thought for a moment. He decided that there could be a simple explanation.

"I expect it was just your mind remembering what happened in November, that's all, Jenny. There's no significance in the black hole. That was probably your body getting ready to wake up. We've all fallen down holes in our dreams."

Jenny seemed comforted by Eddie's interpretation and when he gave her a reassuring hug she left in a reasonably happy mood with Eddie saying finally,

"I will be careful, Jenny. Who would you be able to talk to about complicated and philosophical issues if I wasn't around?"

Jenny didn't know what the second adjective meant but she had got the gist of what her brother was saying.

The school term began in earnest the following day and by the weekend thoughts of ghosts and the forces of good and evil had receded to the back of Eddie's mind. When he had discovered that Sally Barber was not at school on the Friday owing to sickness, he did think that the empty seat beside him in English that afternoon might be filled by his friendly ghost, but Len did not put in an appearance. By the Saturday morning the weather had taken off its mild face and replaced it with a cold and frosty glare. Snow was promised before the weekend was out with forecasters predicting the worst snowfall for three years. Distant memories of a day spent with Len, tobogganing down East Hill, came back to Eddie as he wandered into town that morning with no particular purpose in mind. Though Town had a home league game that afternoon, he had decided to avoid Hamsden and its largest department store in particular. He wasn't ready to face any more encounters with the clashes between good and evil. The previous one had been bad enough and he was scared that, if there was another one, it would be far more difficult to handle.

By the time Eddie reached the junction with Mill Road, a light snow had begun to fall. There was little wind to speak of and the cloud cover above suggested that it was probably going to snow for a very long time. He had read somewhere that, at its worst, snow could pile up at the rate of somewhere between half and a full inch per hour. He pulled the hood of his duffle coat over his head and continued down the High Street towards the sea. It felt good to be walking in the ever-increasing snow and Eddie began to experience an inner peace that he hadn't had for some time. He felt light-headed and almost euphoric as he crossed over the promenade and onto the beach which by then was covered by a good inch of snow. The sea was as calm as a mill pond; it looked oily and strangely inviting. 'Wouldn't it be nice to just walk into it and …?' he thought as he stood right at the sea's edge. Other thoughts of the life that his best friend appeared to enjoy came to Eddie at that melancholic moment. The air was thick with falling snow and visibility out to sea had diminished to less than fifty yards. An eerie silence had descended all around him and as he turned away from the water in an effort to shrug off any more morbid feelings, Eddie was presented with a sight that matched the eeriness he felt both inside his head and in the air that surrounded him. He rubbed his eyes in disbelief. He knew he hadn't drifted off to sleep so this was no nightmare like the last time in the school assembly hall. This had to be real. He knew he had woken up that morning. Suddenly he could hear a voice which was coming from somewhere above him.

"Go home, Eddie. Go home now or you may never get home again."

Eddie looked up into blackness; it had stopped snowing and the sky was dark and brooding. His eyes lowered to the strange sight before him; a sight that he had seen before but had forgotten until then. Fenton-on-Sea had vanished completely and had been replaced by a snowfield of Arctic proportions. It stretched away to the horizon in every direction and was bare of anything, natural or man-made. He turned back to the sea and discovered that the pure white panorama was all-encompassing. His nightmare came back to him fully with one important difference – last time he had woken up out of it in his bed at home.

After Eddie had walked round in a complete circle searching in vain in every direction for landmarks, he suddenly realised that he had completely lost his bearings. Which way was now home – which was the sea? It was pitch black overhead and it was a starless and moonless night. The voice had said for him to make for home straightaway, but where was home? Unlike with the ghosts in Osborne's, this was not a just a choice of two directions – one good, one bad – it was a choice of an infinite number of them. And that was assuming both that the snow would allow him to walk back safely and, more importantly, his home still existed! He walked around for a few moments thinking of what to do. Should he just wait for the scenery to change back? Was this another test of good against evil? Was he the only one who could save himself? Trying to rein in the panic that was forming inside him, he did the only thing possible that he could think of – he fell to his knees and bowed his head to pray.

"O God, please help me get back home. I know that you are the only one who can choose the right direction. Please, please help me!"

After his supplication, Eddie stood up and feigned confidence within himself.

"Show me!" he shouted. "Show me a sign. Make the choice for me."

He waited expectantly. He looked left, then right, then behind him and finally turned to face his original direction. Was that a pinpoint of light on the horizon? He walked forward; the snow was up to his knees. He trudged fifty yards and stopped. The light was brighter and seemed nearer. He tried to run and promptly fell flat on his face in the snow. He crawled forward on all fours and looked again at the source of his possible salvation. He could suddenly make out shapes. He jumped up and ran blindly forward into a fresh blizzard but this time, underfoot, the snow seemed less deep; only up to his ankles. Fortunately within a few yards, he stopped again to try to take in the view ahead. He couldn't believe his eyes. Not more than a hundred yards ahead stood a familiar tall building – St Andrew's Church! He approached with caution. The snow had stopped and now there was barely a covering on the ground. Eddie read the sign outside the main door:

'*PRAISE AND THANK THE LORD ALL WHO ENTER HERE*'

By the time he reached home, Eddie had discovered that time had moved on considerably that Saturday. Though the church clock seemed to indicate that it was nine-thirty, he also knew that it had not been working properly for some time, as, when he reached it, the more reliable one on the station façade indicated ten past three. A quick calculation told Eddie that he had been out for over six hours. At the same time, however, he also realised that he could only really account for about one of them. He was both mentally and physically exhausted. Despite this, he was, at the same time, filled with euphoria and excitement at his remarkable escape from a seemingly impossible situation. He appeared able to call on God at will to save him when in perilous situations. However, this mood was tempered by his mother when he opened the front door of number 38 Fir Tree Close – she had clearly been worried.

"I thought you said you were only going to be an hour or so. Where on earth have you been?"

Eddie hadn't prepared a reason for his lateness; his mind had been on other things on the way home and any invented excuse would have probably not been believed anyway so he said absolutely nothing. He put on his best guilty smile and hoped his mother would draw her own possible romantic conclusion. She did.

"You've been out with a girl, haven't you?"

Again Eddie was silent as he moved past his mum, intending to go straight to his bedroom. His mother persisted gently with her questioning. She actually seemed quite pleased.

"Was it Sally? She's such a nice girl, Eddie."

Eddie halted his progress and turned.

"Yes, Mum."

His mother clearly took the affirmative reply to confirm her suspicions. Eddie, for his part, felt he hadn't actually lied, as his answer could have been interpreted as merely being an agreement with his mum's simple assessment of the suitability of Sally Barber. He completed the escape to his bedroom unaware that his mother would probably never again question his movements too closely. As far as she was concerned, her only son was in love.

Eddie didn't eat much for the rest of Saturday. His lack of an appetite fitted perfectly with his mother's conclusions and so she didn't disturb him. For his part, he spent much of the time until he went to bed, thinking about the morning's events. He found it, at the same time, both worrying and exciting that Len had not been party to his escape from an impossible situation. As on a previous occasion, Eddie was beginning to sense that he had been privileged to 'look behind the curtain' and gain a glimpse and knowledge of a world where God was truly in charge as good and evil fought each other on a daily basis. The question that kept coming back to him, however, was: 'Why?' He would have to debate this with Len the next time he appeared.

23

Wrong Choice

It was to be another couple of weeks before Len would pay Eddie another visit and it was under unfamiliar circumstances when he did. Sally Barber's illness had been a short-lived stomach bug and she had quickly returned to school on the Monday after Eddie's adventure in the snow. Eddie's mother continued to smile knowingly at him whenever he was late from school or elsewhere. Eddie was happy to go along with the charade whenever it suited his purpose and he needed a silent excuse to cover it. By Friday, January the 21st, he had almost given up hope of Len appearing again, especially when the adjacent seat in English was always occupied by Miss Barber.

The afternoon English lesson became a very trying experience for Eddie. On three separate occasions he had given wrong answers to Mr Green's questions despite some helpful prompting from Sally beside him. In the end, Mr Green decided to leave him alone for the last ten minutes of the lesson, concentrating instead on the brighter pupils at the front of the class. At the end of the lesson, Eddie found that Sally appeared to want to accompany him on part of his walk home. Though such a thing had happened occasionally in the past, it had always been by chance and not by design as he thought on that afternoon.

Once they were walking in South Road and had exchanged and exhausted their views on the afternoon's lesson, Sally changed subject abruptly taking Eddie completely by surprise.

"Are you doing anything tomorrow?"

He was awkward and diffident with his reply.

"Er, I don't know. Er, I don't think so. I suppose I might be going out sometime."

"*Make up your mind, mate. She's about to ask you out.*"

Eddie glanced to his right to see Len walking boldly in step with the two teenagers. Sally continued unaware of the invisible interloper.

"Well, if you're not, I was wondering if you'd like to go to Hamsden to do some shopping and so on."

"*Ask her what she means by 'so on', Eddie?*"

Eddie ignored Len's facetious question and said,

"Maybe. I'll have to check with my mum first, Sally. I'll give you a ring later, if that's O.K."

Sally looked disappointed at Eddie's non-committal response but she smiled sweetly enough and replied,

"Fine – you've got my number, haven't you?"

"Yes," he lied and then, to his great embarrassment, she came right up to him and planted a kiss on his cheek. She then skipped and ran her way down South Road towards the High Street. Len burst out laughing.

"Well, you *are* a dark horse and no mistake, mate. She fancies you, old boy. Not a bad looker as well."

Eddie moved to a low wall where he sat down as though watching the traffic pass by. Len sat beside him.

"Stop it, Len," said Eddie. "It's bad enough having to deal with a lovesick girl without you playing gooseberry as well."

"Sorry, Captain. I thought you'd be alone on your walk home. I was going to take you on a day out tomorrow but I can see you're going to be otherwise engaged."

In the distance Eddie thought he could just make out Sally turning and waving back at him. He was beginning to feel pressurised and pulled two different ways at once with equally attractive choices. However, he made an instant decision. He could see Sally anytime and he hadn't made a commitment to her anyway whilst Len might not be able to come back for some time.

"No problem, Len. I'll come with you. Anyway, who wants to go shopping …?"

He didn't finish the sentence with 'with a girl' as somewhere deep inside he was actually incredibly flattered by Sally's invitation but his love life could wait, couldn't it?

"Are you sure, mate?"

"Yes, certain. I see Sally everyday at school. What did you have in mind for tomorrow, Len?"

"You'll have to wait until the morning for the destination. Let's just say it's somewhere that neither of us has ever been before."

"Really? That sounds exotic."

Len grinned and said finally,

"Be outside the station no later than eight-thirty in the morning."

"Are we going by train, then?" asked Eddie excitedly but as soon as he had phrased the question, Len vanished before his eyes.

Eddie couldn't find the Barbers' telephone number when he looked later that evening; they were ex-directory. He decided he would apologise to Sally when he saw her at school on Monday. She would understand.

Eddie slept fitfully that night as a mixture of guilt and excitement fought for his attention. In the end, visions of fabulous cities and island paradises won the day and the sleep that eventually came extended until just after eight o'clock. He had to wash and dress quickly when he realised he had overslept so badly. Grabbing some toast and a coffee, he was barely able to respond to his mum's question.

"Where are you off to in such a hurry, Eddie? Got a date?"

Ann Compton could tell by the look on her son's face that she was correct in her assumption. As Eddie bolted for the front door and, between mouthfuls of toast and marmite, he managed to say,

"See you later, Mum. I don't know when we'll be back."

Whether it was a Freudian slip or not, his mum didn't get the chance to say, 'I knew it, Eddie. I just knew it'; her son was already halfway down the front path.

Despite his late awakening, Eddie was only seven minutes late arriving at the station, but he cursed himself when he realised that, in his haste, he had not brought any money with him. To make matters worse, Len was nowhere to be seen. When the station clock displayed a quarter to nine, he decided to check inside the station to see if he could find his friend's ghost. He knew he had until at least ten past if Len was proposing to go by train to Hamsden. He avoided passing the ticket office where his dad would be at work and checked as much of the two platforms as he could. With very few people about, it was easy for Eddie to decide that Len was not in the station or at least, if he was, he wasn't showing himself. Eddie wandered disconsolately, head down, out of the station.

"Oh good, you have decided to come, Eddie. I bet you didn't have my phone number after all."

Eddie looked up to see an impossible nightmare standing before him. Sally Barber was accompanied by another girl who Eddie thought he recognised as another pupil from Fenton Grammar. Eddie thought hurriedly.

"Can't stop, Sally, I've got to go back home; I've forgotten something. I'll catch the later train and see you in Pritchard's for coffee at about eleven, O.K?"

"Ye-yes, O.K.," stammered Sally. Her friend looked amused. Eddie ran out into the station forecourt and didn't stop until he had made the High Street out of the sight of either girl. He paused for breath and realised that he had been fortunate. He was also glad for Sally that he hadn't ruined her day and that she had still been able to go to Hamsden with someone. He would worry on Monday about a reason for not being able to join her for coffee though.

When Eddie heard the familiar noise of the ten past nine train making its way out of Fenton station, he made his way back to the forecourt still hoping to find Len waiting for him. When he discovered that there was no sign of him, he began to think that he had made the wrong choice for his day out. The next train to Hamsden was at twenty to the hour and it didn't take him long to resolve to take it if Len's ghost hadn't shown by then. Being entertained by two girls didn't seem too bad a substitute for a ghostly trip, no matter how exotic.

The next train duly arrived and Eddie boarded it as planned. He was cross both with himself for being late, but also with Len for not waiting just a few short minutes longer. The train went straight through to Hamsden; Linham junction had raised Eddie's hopes but the nine-forty did not stop there on a Saturday. Walking into town, Eddie became a little nervous at the thought of meeting up with Sally and her friend; he knew he wasn't experienced with girls. He silently wished that Len's ghost would still appear and to that end, he toyed with the idea of going to Osborne's. However, he quickly dismissed the thought from his mind; he didn't want to be faced with more impossible choices.

He had just reached the town centre proper when some glossy posters caught his eye in a shop window. East Shires Travel was advertising all their summer holidays to places far and wide. Gorgeous technicolour views of Paris, New York and Rome shouted at the more well-heeled passers-by. To pass the time and delay a visit to Pritchard's Coffee House, Eddie began to imagine himself going to any of the three destinations. He tried to decide which one he would like to visit first. Rome won the day; he and Len had been to Paris and the Big Apple looked too brash and busy for his taste. Architecture like that of the Colliseum appealed to Eddie much more than skyscrapers and the like. He could also recall some phrases that he'd learned in Geography or History at school: 'Rome wasn't built in a day'; 'When in Rome, do as the Romans do' and, most appropriate for him 'All roads lead to Rome'. There was a fourth one but it escaped him at that moment; it couldn't be important, he decided. Yes, he thought, it would be nice to go to the Eternal City. Even the very name fitted in with his recent experience of the everlasting fight between good and evil.

"And that's precisely where I was going to take us until you didn't turn up on time like I asked."

Eddie didn't know how long his friendly ghost had been standing beside him or that he could read his thoughts too. He quickly did his security check of the ghost's identity and when all was well, he said,

"I was only a few minutes late, Len."

"I know, mate, but it was fun watching you agonise over what you should do. It'll teach you to be late in future, eh?"

"You mean you were just playing with me?"

"A bit – I did wonder what you would do if I didn't show up."

"You've been following me as well?"

"Yes, but you would never have seen me; I was too well hidden. When you reached the travel agents, I could sense what you were thinking and you actually started talking to yourself, believe it or not."

Eddie raised his eyebrows.

"What did I say?"

"Something about all roads leading to Rome."

Eddie said nothing further as it seemed that his friendly ghost had already started preparing *his* 'road' to the Eternal City. Len's face was a mask of concentration and within a few seconds, Eddie was plunged into the familiar darkness and absolute silence.

It was a beautiful spring morning when normal light returned. The Italian capital was at its finest with the pink almond blossom in full bloom. Flower sellers pushed their handcarts full of mimosa and violets and the air was heady with scent. As Eddie looked around him, he marvelled at the splendour of one of the most beautiful cities in the world. He and Len were sitting in one of the many parks in the city and it was mid-morning judging by the position of the sun overhead. No one would take any notice of the lone young boy talking to himself in a foreign language after Len began the conversation.

"What do you think, then? I thought I'd choose May; it's such a nice month and …."

"And?"

"And three years ago this month we thought we were going there on our first fantastic journey. Do you remember?"

"Vaguely – you must have a good memory."

"Certain things come back to me more clearly now that I'm dead."

Eddie looked puzzled.

"Did you say three years ago?"

"Yes, it was late May 1963, I believe."

"But when I left Hamsden it was only January the 22nd."

"Yes," said Len. "We've moved forward in time but only by about four months. You've done that before, Eddie."

"Not with you as a ghost though. That's a bit scarier, Len."

"Not as long as I'm with you, but …."

"I knew there would be a 'but'."

"But I have an extra surprise for you."

"What?"

"While you're in the future you're invisible to everyone except for me. You're my trainee ghost. You have an advantage over me as well."

"Oh yeah. What?"

"You still have your real body. If you didn't have it you'd be a full ghost and you know what that would mean."

Eddie looked down at himself.

"Go on," said Len. "Feel yourself."

Eddie pinched his own left arm and then slapped both thighs. He laughed out loud.

"I'm real and invisible. It's magic, Len – absolute ruddy magic."

"Yes it is, but be careful. Because you have a real body you can still get hurt or even drown, so don't go falling off any bridges or the like. No one would be able to help you because they wouldn't be able to see you."

Edoardo Giordano drove a *camion rifiuti* for his living; he was a good and honest garbage disposal expert – a dustman. His job was to visit some of Rome's central parks to collect the tons of rubbish from the hundreds of bins located there. He lived about eight miles out of the city not far from the recycling and waste disposal plant where he took his truck at the end of each day. Though his cargo was often smelly as well as dirty, he was proud that he kept the paintwork of his truck in pristine condition. It was thus with some surprise and disappointment that, when he checked it at the end of that late spring day, he found the front bumper and grill had sustained some damage. There were several small dents and scratches on the surface of the metal. He was certain he hadn't come into contact with anything that day and thus it was a complete mystery to him how they had got there. There was no trace of animal hair or bird feathers; it was not uncommon to have fatal arguments with the wildlife on the country roads near the disposal plant. He also decided that it would have had to have been a fairly large animal to have caused such damage. In the end he thought it could only have been caused by another vehicle reversing into his truck while he had left it unattended.

24

Another Eden

Eddie made two tragic but human mistakes in his eagerness to see Italy's capital; one before he set off and one during his all too brief visit there. He forgot that Italian drivers use the right side of the road and not the left, which, combined with the broadness of some thoroughfares, meant that he should have exercised extra care when crossing one to rush to see one of the city's sights. He never saw his namesake and his big red truck and, just before the fatal moment, he was reminded of his other mistake in not recalling the fourth clichéd phrase concerning the Eternal City. 'See Rome and die' might just have swayed his choice of day out back to the safety of Pritchard's Coffee House and the promise of his first relationship with a member of the opposite sex. These two mistakes, however, actually disguised a more fundamental reason for his wrong choice for a day out. On occasions before, when faced with much more difficult and frightening choices, Eddie had sought help from the God in whom he put his trust. On the more mundane matter he had neglected to do so, choosing to take his own judgement over divine counsel.

For Eddie's part, however, he had found contentment and his friendship with Len had been restored to completeness for eternity. From then on he would be able to see and communicate with him whenever he wanted to. As Len had told him in the past, he wouldn't grow old, or tired, or hungry. He wouldn't need money or clothes or somewhere to live. He wouldn't need to get angry or jealous or sad. He would never be scared again and he wouldn't need to sleep. He would exist forever as a happy fourteen-year-old in a world that was peaceful and ordered. Above all, he would never have to worry about man's biggest fear ever again.

When he didn't return to his home in Fenton-on-Sea that cold January day, the emergency services would make their statutory searches but sadly, of course, without success. Sally Barber would report later that she had seen Eddie running away from Fenton station and that he was going to meet her later in Hamsden. It would turn out that she had been the last person to see him as nobody else reported a sighting of him afterwards. A few months later and the powers that be would declare that Edward James Compton was posted as officially missing, presumed dead. That assumed verdict would not be finalised for another seven years. Some people, Eddie's mum and sister included, formed the opinion that he had never really been the same since his best friend had been tragically killed in a car accident. They consoled themselves and others with the hope that the two boys' special friendship had been rekindled for eternity.

www.ingramcontent.com/pod-product-compliance
Lightning Source LLC
Chambersburg PA
CBHW020829260626
47169CB00003B/907